AFTER

FRANCINE PROSE

AFTER

JOANNA COTLER BOOKS

An Imprint of HarperCollins*Publishers*

Library of Congress Cataloging-in-Publication Data

Prose, Francine.

After / by Francine Prose.— 1st ed.

p. cm.

Summary: In the aftermath of a nearby school shooting, a grief and crisis counselor takes over Central High School and enacts increasingly harsh measures to control students, while those who do not comply disappear.

ISBN 0-06-008081-7 — ISBN 0-06-008082-5 (lib. bdg.)

[1. School shootings—Fiction. 2. High Schools—Fiction. 3. Schools—Fiction. 4. Conspiracies—Fiction.] I. Title.

PZ7.P94347 Af 2003   2002014386

[Fic]—dc21   CIP

                                                                                        AC

Typography by Alicia Mikles

1 2 3 4 5 6 7 8 9 10

First Edition

For Bruno and Leon

MINUTES AFTER THE SHOOTINGS, everybody's cell phone rang. We weren't supposed to have cell phones unless we had a note from our parents explaining why they had to be able to reach us in a hurry.

But most of us had them anyway, and, as it turned out, most of the parents (for all their complaining about how much TV *kids* watched) were close enough to a radio or television so that they found out immediately, and all the phones went off at once. The annoying rings and the stupid songs sang out, only slightly muffled, from inside everyone's backpacks.

I was relieved that mine didn't ring first. By the time my dad reached me, practically everyone in the class had a phone pressed to one ear and a finger in the other. Mrs. Davis, our algebra teacher, had given up trying to keep order and was just trying to listen in because it was clear, even to her, that something awful had happened.

My dad said, "Tomster! Are you okay?"

I said, "Don't call me that. Why wouldn't I be? What's *with* you? I'm in math class."

After a silence my dad said, "I thought you hated math."

"So?" I said. "So what?"

"So what's the big deal about my interrupting?"

"Earth to Dad," I said. I imagined him in his studio, in the barn behind our house, surrounded by piles of papers and drawings and little bottles of ink. He always said that I never paid any attention to what he was working on, but in fact I knew that his current project involved illustrating a cookbook about the different ways to cook beans. International beans from around the world. "What's going on?"

He said, "I've got some really bad news. Some crazy kids shot up the school gym at Pleasant Valley and killed a bunch of students and teachers."

"Oh, man," I said. "That *is* really bad. But Dad . . . that's fifty miles away. I'm in math class."

"I don't know. Sorry," said Dad. "I got worried. I wanted to make sure you were okay."

There were three killers. Two boys and a girl. No one even knew they were friends, let alone that they'd been plotting to bring a whole arsenal into the school and go on a murder spree. They never even registered as blips on the other kids' radar screens.

The TV news made a big point of that, long before anyone was even sure how many students and teachers were dead, or exactly who had been killed. Those details took longer to come out. Five kids and three teachers had been shot dead on the spot. Fourteen students were critically wounded. The killers all shot themselves. The one girl killer left a note on her computer at home saying she wasn't sorry for what she had done except for the heartache and trouble that this was probably going to cause her mom and dad. *Probably?* I'd say *definitely*.

Most of the kids they shot were in the gym. They hunted down the jocks. As they flashed the faces of the dead on the screen, it was horribly depressing. They must have killed all the best-looking kids, the most handsome and photogenic.

The fact that they'd mostly killed athletes really gave me the creeps. Because in our school, me and my friends—Brian, Avery, and Silas—we *were* the jocks. Except we were a subclique of jocks. The Smart Jocks—that's what everyone called us. Not that we were outstandingly smart. Except for Brian and sometimes Avery, we weren't especially good in school, plus we weren't that jocky. We could play basketball passably well. But calling us the Smart Jocks set us apart from the Dumb Jocks, who were *certifiably* dumb, and also from the Brains, none of whom could even have made the junior basketball team.

Also we were known as rebels. Sort of. Because there wasn't much to rebel *against*, we never got into actual trouble. And it wasn't *exactly* that we had a bad attitude. It was more that we needed to cultivate the *appearance* of having a bad attitude. We always sat in the back rows—on the bus, in class, during assembly. We were the first to roll our eyes when a teacher said something corny. And no one expected us to offer our services when, say, at the end of ninth grade, they'd asked kids to volunteer to be Big Brothers for next year's incoming freshmen. Not that we were completely lacking in community spirit. But, as Silas said, who wanted to waste the best two weeks of school—those few days when you could still imagine that the year might be interesting and fun—showing some little dweeb how to open his locker and where the bathrooms were?

And it was fine, no one expected us to volunteer, that was one good thing about Central. Everyone had a place; you were allowed to be who you were. I mean, *whoever* you were. It was totally live and let live. But after Pleasant Valley, all that began to change. You started looking at other kids differently. Because the nasty lesson of Pleasant Valley was that kids you never thought about, kids you hardly even *noticed* . . . well, they could be thinking about *you* all the time, they could hate you and plan to *kill* you. Which turned out to have been their problem: No one ever noticed them until they started shooting.

By the time we heard for ourselves about the killings at Pleasant Valley, school was closed, and we were home watching the news. We called and e-mailed back and forth. We couldn't believe that it had happened in a place which, under the circumstances, had such a cruel joke of a name. Someone said the town was going to change its name to Death Valley, but nobody thought that was funny, especially when the TV started showing, over and over and over, footage of the emergency medical teams and the state troopers carrying out

6

all those stretchers with blankets pulled all the way up. After a while, I didn't want to watch, but I couldn't stop watching.

That evening, when my dad came inside from his studio, he didn't even complain about my watching TV. He sat down and watched the news with me. We didn't say anything. We didn't have to.

For dinner, we heated up some frozen enchiladas, which was what he usually bought for my dinner when he was planning to go out with his girlfriend, Clara. So I assumed that he must have had a date with Clara and canceled because of Pleasant Valley.

He said, "Tom, do you want to talk?"

I said, "Sure, Dad. About what?"

"About how upsetting and tragic this is."

"It's terrible," I said. "I don't know what to say—"

"How are the enchiladas?" he said.

I could never bring myself to tell him that I hated frozen enchiladas. When he was out with

Clara, sometimes I took my plate out to the yard and dumped them out at the far edge of the lawn where I thought the raccoons might get them. The enchiladas depressed me. It was the kind of thing my dad did sometimes, the kind of thing that was supposed to cheer me up. He acted as if heating up frozen enchiladas was some bad-boy thing that we could do on our own now, a rebel thing that we could never have done when my mom was alive, because she might have disapproved.

Mom was a great cook, so I suppose it was true. She just wouldn't have gotten the point of frozen Mexican food. Mom died four years ago, in an auto wreck. She drove terribly, but slowly, so we didn't think it mattered. We never imagined that you could get killed going forty miles an hour and running into a tree when you reached down to get your favorite Charlie Parker tape. Anyway, the point was, the enchiladas sucked.

"They're fine," I said. "I mean, they're delicious."

Dad said, "Should I worry that you're closing

down and hiding your real feelings?"

That didn't sound like my dad at all. He'd never said anything like that even when my mom died. In fact, he always made fun of people who said things like sharing and caring and getting in touch with your anger. I said, "Where did you get *that*?"

"Television," said Dad. "Plus I got an e-mail from school telling us we should be monitoring you kids for signs of withdrawal and depression."

"School *e-mailed* you?" I said. That was something new. All the students were on e-mail and probably all the teachers, too. But the school was old-fashioned; they still used snail mail when they wanted to get in touch with the parents. They sent out calendars and team schedules, just the pages, stapled to save money on envelopes and postage.

"A very long message," he said. "Dress code violations will no longer be tolerated."

"Yeah, right," I said. I reached across the table and squeezed his shoulder. I said, "Want to know my real feelings, Dad? My real feelings are: I wish it hadn't happened. And my other real feeling is: I'm glad it didn't happen at Central."

School was closed the next day. There were a couple of bomb scares, which was nothing new; there were a couple of those every year. But now they had to take everything seriously. They were concerned about copycat crime, though that didn't make sense since the killings at Pleasant Valley had nothing to do with bombs.

By the time we got back on Wednesday, morning classes were delayed for an all-school assembly to introduce us to Dr. Willner, our new grief and crisis counselor. When Ms. Baker, my homeroom teacher, announced we were having assembly, some kids cheered and whistled. They were scheduled to have a first-period English quiz, and now they were going to miss it.

In the auditorium I looked for Silas and Brian and Avery, but they were sitting toward the back, and the back filled up right away. I couldn't believe they hadn't saved me a seat.

"Thanks," I told them, and sat in the middle between two girls I didn't know. Central High had more than five hundred students, and all of them just about fit into the auditorium, which was one of those old-fashioned theaters that slanted down toward a huge raised stage with a flag and velvet curtains.

On the stage were two chairs. Mr. Trent, our principal, sat in one, and the new guy sat in the other. Mr. Trent always looked so self-conscious and nervous that it was hard to see any difference when, after the kids finally quieted down, he rose and shuffled forward—with that hunched, pigeon-toed walk of his—and tiptoed up to the podium.

He said, "The killings at Pleasant Valley are upsetting and tragic for us all."

Funny. *Upsetting* and *tragic* were the same words my dad had used.

"And I know that our hearts and our prayers

went out to all the students and teachers and parents at Pleasant Valley."

By some miracle my friends and I had made it all the way to sophomore year without being called into Mr. Trent's office. But we knew kids who had, including a friend of Silas's who'd been busted by the soccer coach for drinking a beer behind the bleachers. He said that halfway through lecturing him and threatening him with suspension, Mr. Trent had seemed to forget his name and what exactly he'd done wrong. Still, even though we made fun of Mr. Trent, we knew we had a good deal. Everyone had heard horror stories about school principals who acted like the prison warden in some old movie you'd catch on TV at three o'clock in the morning.

Going to sleep the night before, I'd been trying to think if I actually knew any kids who went to Pleasant Valley. We'd played them in basketball, twice. Once we lost, and once we won. At least I thought so. I could hardly remember the games.

Mr. Trent said, "These are troubling times, anxious and confusing. And our school, our little community, needs all the help it can get. It's our very good fortune that the state of Massachusetts has generously set aside funds to provide us with the benefits of trained, professional guidance."

He paused and said, "And now it's my great pleasure to introduce you to Dr. Henry Willner. Dr. Willner is a former professor of clinical psychology who has generously given up a college teaching career to come down and work in the trenches with high-school kids in crisis. Dr. Willner will be with us at Central High for the next three months, making himself available to students who would like his help, meeting with us individually and in small groups, helping the school get back on track and, of course, making certain that nothing like the tragic events at Pleasant Valley ever happens here."

Dr. Willner was very tall, with a beard. He looked a little like Abraham Lincoln, but without the sweet-natured saintly part. Once when I was little, and my mom was still alive, we all went down to Disney World, where we watched an Abraham Lincoln robot stand up and walk across the stage and deliver the Gettysburg Address. It scared me so badly I burst into tears. I never forgot it, and now I almost felt as if the demon robot had been looking for me all these years and at last it had found me.

All of Dr. Willner's motions were sharp and abrupt—actually, kind of robotic. He stood and walked to the podium, trying to make eye contact with as many kids as he could, staring steadily into the crowd as if he were our best friend, when the fact was that he'd just gotten there. He was a stranger, he didn't know us.

He said, "With the killings at Pleasant Valley, we have entered a new era. Monday, we were children, but today we are grown-ups with all the griefs and responsibilities that come along with adulthood. We have learned that something like that can happen right in our midst—no longer just to other people, other teachers and students, far away in Colorado and Kentucky. It can happen in our own backyard, here in western Massachusetts."

I thought it was strange he said that. I'd been moody and spooked for days after the killings happened at Columbine and Paducah. The idea it happened *anywhere* was really sad and upsetting. But this didn't really make it seem so much worse—that is, the fact that it happened nearby. If anything, it seemed to improve our odds that it wouldn't happen at Central, like the odds against lightning striking twice in the same place. In a way, I guess, you could say that Pleasant Valley took the bullet—the bullets—for us.

But that wasn't how Dr. Willner's mind worked. The nearness of Pleasant Valley seemed to make a big difference to him.

He said, "We can no longer pretend to ourselves that it can't happen here. And so we must change our lifestyle to keep our community safe and make sure that it *won't* happen. It means sharing our feelings, becoming better people. Beginning the hard work of healing and recovery. Working through our fear and grief. And in the process maybe giving up some of the privileges that we may have taken for granted. I am afraid that circumstances make it a virtual certainty that some of the privileges that we all have enjoyed may have to be taken away."

It was all I could do then not to twist around and look for Silas and Brian and Avery and see if they had heard that. Did the guy just say we were going to lose our privileges? What privileges did he mean? Mostly when parents said something like that—which my dad hardly ever did—it meant you couldn't watch TV or hang out all night on the phone or the Internet. And when kids screwed up and totaled the family station wagon, they got their car keys taken away. So what was this guy *thinking*, saying that to an auditorium full of teenagers who were very familiar with the concept of losing privileges? Was Dr. Willner telling us that the whole school was going to be *grounded*?

He said, "Already there is convincing evidence that illegal drugs were involved in the shootings at Pleasant Valley, which, as you all know, were done with handguns and high-powered automatic weapons. For that reason, Central is adopting— as of today—a Zero Tolerance policy toward substance abuse and weapons possession. One infraction means that you will be expelled with no possibility of readmission."

Somebody in the back of the auditorium made a loud sucking sound, like someone smoking a joint. A couple of kids burst out laughing, and then suddenly quit laughing.

Dr. Willner stopped cold—and again looked into the crowd. His beady glare seemed to make its way straight back through that huge auditorium, seat by seat, row by row, one student at a time. And maybe I was imagining things, but it seemed to me then that Mr. Willner's eyes snagged on mine for a moment, and hovered there for a long scary beat, until he blinked and moved on.

Finally he fixed us all with his most melting, supersympathetic look, a look that would have been more convincing if not for that cold, angry gleam in his eyes.

He said, "I'm sure we will get to know one another as we work together to make sure that we here at Central High have a peaceful and happy future."

By the time I hooked up with my friends in the second-floor corridor, we were all fixated on the part about losing privileges. It was wrong, it wasn't fair. Why should *we* lose anything because some lunatics went ballistic at a school fifty miles away? A couple of girls said we should trust the school, the school knew what it was doing, the school probably knew best. And there were even some guys who said, "Look at it this way. You can't be too careful." Also, I remember a few kids actually saying, "We should do whatever they tell us. It's for our own safety and protection. Maybe we think it won't happen here . . . but that's what the kids at Pleasant Valley thought. Until it happened there."

"You know what it makes me want to do?" Brian said. "It makes me want to buy a gun and bring it into school." Our laughs were strained, though we knew Brian was kidding. Of all of us four, Brian got the best grades and was the best-looking. All the teachers loved him. But no one held that against him. Girls were always calling him up, he was a very popular guy, maybe because he was always saying outrageous, wicked stuff like that.

"It makes me want to get high," said Silas. "I mean, so totally *loaded* that I can start to see the sense in what this Willner dude is saying." Briefly I wondered if he was the one who'd made the joint-sucking sound in the back of auditorium. But that seemed unlikely. He couldn't afford to take the chance.

Silas was a serious stoner. He was the only one of us who regularly came to school high. But the strangest thing was that, despite what you would have thought, smoking helped Silas's basketball game—especially his foul shot. Still, he was always paranoid. He believed that the silliest, most unrelated things were part of some secret plot, and he was always finding evidence to prove that nothing was what it appeared on the surface. A lot of his ideas were hilarious. He'd say, "You know that car ad on TV with those hot chicks singing along in the SUV? Well, I heard that if you listen hard to the lyrics, it turns out there's this encrypted message from the CIA."

Now Avery said, "Maybe we're all getting totally fried over nothing. Probably we should just chill out and let this whole *privileges* thing blow over. I mean, you know how grown-ups are. They've basically got the attention spans of a fruit fly. By next week, they'll forget about it. This Willner dude will be history."

Everyone agreed that Avery was going to become a lawyer, or run for Congress, or work for a newspaper someday. There was nothing in the world that Avery liked better than getting information and forming an opinion and then arguing until he'd bored you to death. On the other hand, he was really good at figuring out logically what would happen next, which was mostly why Coach Pete picked him to play point guard when we got to play in a game. Avery was the only black kid on the basketball team, which wasn't so strange, really, because there were only a couple dozen black kids in the entire school. They mostly hung out together, they sat at the same table at lunch. And I guess it must have been a problem for Avery that he hung out with us. But we never talked about it—the whole subject made us uncomfortable. Every so often, Avery would say, "*The white man* this and that," or "*white people* this and that." And we'd give him a hard time about it. We'd say, "That is just so *racist*."

Silas said, "*What* privileges? Like, what have we got to lose, man? Because, face it, from the time we get on the school bus till the time it drops us back at our houses, we basically have to do whatever the most retarded teacher tells us. But still . . . they'd love to get us to the point where we are like, basically, slaves. Did you know that the pyramids were mostly built by kids?"

Brian said, "Silas, man, you are *so* paranoid. You've *got* to lay off that weed."

The four of us stood in the hall, while the others moved around us like a stream dividing and flowing around a big boulder in the middle. We were a clique in a school of cliques. Like every high school, I imagined. Pleasant Valley, the TV news kept saying, was also a cliquey school. The kids who'd done the killings belonged to the clique of not belonging.

The four of us had only one class together—as it happened, the only class we liked. Social studies. Mrs. Ridley would usually let us spend the first part of class talking about things that bothered or interested us, mostly things we'd seen on the news.

The four of us sat in the back of the room. That was fine with Mrs. Ridley. She knew we'd mostly pay attention. Often she counted on Brian to be the first to talk when she started the class by asking, "Is there anyone who would like to bring up a topic of general interest?"

That question was her trademark. She said it all the time. We imitated her saying it, but the truth was, we liked it.

But that day she stood up front and said, "I'm sure you're all as thrilled as I am that Dr. Willner has come to Central to help us sort through our feelings of grief and loss."

Thrilled? Sort through our feelings of grief and loss? That didn't sound like Mrs. Ridley. Silas and I caught each other's eyes.

"Would anyone like to share?" said Mrs. Ridley. "Would anyone like to reach out about the tragic events at Pleasant Valley?"

Share? Reach out? It sounded like my dad talking about hiding my real feelings.

Anyway, none of us was going for it. We had other things on our minds.

No one said anything for a long time. And then Becca Sawyer, the class kiss-up, who always sat in the front row, who never criticized anything, who never talked out of turn, who never passed a note or got anything less than an A plus, said, "Excuse me, but I don't understand why the Central High kids are about to lose our privileges when we didn't *do* anything wrong."

Everyone said, "Yeah, that's right." "That's right." "What's the deal here?"

Becca looked back and beamed at the class. She'd never gotten that kind of approval before.

"Excuse me," said Mrs. Ridley. "Class, you have to be quiet." What had gotten into her? That didn't sound like her, either. Because ordinarily Mrs. Ridley waded into the middle of the classroom and stood between the desks and spun her hands in propeller circles, as if she were literally trying to churn up our minds, to get us thinking, to keep our thoughts rolling, to see how we could reason, and where our reasoning could take us.

But that day she stood at the front of the room with her arms straight down at her sides. She said, "Actually, I'm not sure it's entirely appropriate for us to discuss this in this class. In just a few days, I promise you, we should all know more about what the administration has in mind. For the present, if you have any questions about school policy, I urge you all to take them up with Mr. Trent or Dr. Willner."

This time, I didn't even have to look at Silas or Brian or Avery.

It had only been two weeks since Silas and Avery made Brian and me watch *Invasion of the Body Snatchers*. Silas and Avery had rented the tape, they'd watched it twice, and then Silas had bought a copy on the Internet. We screened it in Brian's basement, late one Saturday night when we were all staying over at his house. And it had really spooked us, with its funky '50s camerawork, its *Night of the Living Dead* black and white. For just a moment it crossed my mind that Mrs. Ridley had been taken over by . . .

I told myself to get a grip. I was starting to think like Silas.

two

*T*HAT MORNING, AS SOON AS we got off the bus, we could tell that something was different. A line of kids snaked out the front door as if they were waiting to buy tickets to a rock concert.

The school must have worked all through the night. Because by morning, they'd installed metal detectors—like two chirping toy soldiers guarding every door. They'd also hired people to inspect students' backpacks. The guards didn't stop and search everyone, but they'd stare at you as you went by, and if they didn't like your looks, they'd ask you to step out of line, and pretty soon they'd be going through every crumpled tissue and beat-up old candy wrapper.

How could they have hired anyone so fast? Maybe the guards came with Dr. Willner, maybe they were part of the team sent by the state to work with—what had Mr. Trent said?—high-school kids in crisis. Except that we *weren't* in crisis. We just had metal detectors.

Brian said, "Wait here, guys," and cut the line all the way to the front. He was the only one of us who could have gotten away with doing that without getting killed. He disappeared inside the front door, then came back a few minutes later.

"It's way bizarre in there," Brian reported. "Very orderly, very quiet. There's this sign that says that anyone who obstructs the security process will be sent directly to the principal's office and will receive a minimum one-day mandatory suspension. So everybody's completely shut down and obedient, and everyone's just filing through these nasty metal detectors. Like cattle. Some kids are having to go through back and forth several times. And then they're getting swiped with those sonar cancer paddles, some kids are getting their backpacks opened and checked—"

"Like the airport," Avery said.

"Worse than the airport," Brian said. "Like going to the airport *every morning*, and you don't even get to travel anywhere."

"Oh, man," said Silas. "This is bad news. I can't believe they just *did* this without at least giving us some kind of warning." He started fishing around in his backpack and finally grabbed something and pulled it out and tossed it like a tiny, high-speed Frisbee into the scraggly brownish shrubs pressing up against the school. Fortunately we were the only ones who saw him ditch his stash, and even we pretended we didn't notice. I watched Silas follow it with his eyes. I hoped he wasn't going to come back later and try to find the joint, or whatever it was.

Avery said, "It's like I keep saying. This can't last. They'll keep this up for a couple weeks, and there won't be any more shootings, at least not around here, and they'll get sick of it, lose interest, give it up. It's way too expensive. They've got budget problems as it is."

I wanted to believe Avery. But waiting outside on the steps was putting me in a foul mood. I kept thinking of a line in a blues song my mom used to listen to: "*You don't miss your water till your well runs dry.*" I often thought how true it was, about all kinds of things. And now that we were standing around, waiting to get searched, only now did I miss what I hadn't even known enough to appreciate: being able to just walk through the door and go right into school. It was hard to believe that it had been like that only yesterday. Because already yesterday seemed like years ago. On the very first day we had metal detectors, it seemed as if we'd had them forever.

"No, man," said Silas. "This is just the beginning. The first day of the rest of our lives." He snorted. "Like, they've been wanting to do this all along, and Pleasant Valley was just the excuse they finally needed to start checking up and searching us and following us and tapping our phones. . . ."

Silas and Avery had been having this conversation nonstop for the past few days. I looked at Brian, who rolled his eyes.

"Silas," said Brian. "How much of your stash did you eat before you threw the rest in the bushes?"

"None," said Silas. "Not a bit. Man, I've never been straighter."

Taking tiny baby steps, we inched our way up the stairs. We were going to be late for homeroom. Well, too bad. So would everyone else. If they were going to do this, they should have worked it out with the bus companies to get here fifteen minutes earlier. Which would mean . . . *waking up fifteen minutes earlier*. I knew that this was a minor inconvenience compared to what happened at Pleasant Valley, but still, I didn't have to like it.

Finally we got through the doors and stood in the steamy vestibule, holding the door open behind us until a fat middle-aged guy in a uniform came out from inside the school and asked us to shut the door. Obviously we shut it. The guy was twice my size. There were three guards at this one entrance alone.

Looking through the second set of doors, I watched a guy from my second-period biology class going back and forth through the metal detectors and taking off his wristwatch and going through them again. In, out, in, out, *bleep bleep*, it kept going off. What were they planning to do about the fact that a quarter of the school wore braces? Have a resident dentist stationed at each door to unwire and rewire you every time you had to go through the metal detectors?

By this point the guy was a total wreck, but he was having a wonderful time compared to Becca Sawyer, whom they'd stopped for a random check. Which goes to show how much they knew about the school if they were searching *her*. Then the thought crossed my mind that somehow maybe they *did* know that Becca was the one who'd spoken up in Mrs. Ridley's class yesterday and said that it was unfair that we might lose our privileges for nothing. Silas's paranoia was starting to get to me again. Because probably the truth was that the little dried-up woman in a uniform just didn't like Becca's face.

She made Becca empty out her backpack on the counter. Then she took her time as she casually poked through the pile of Tampaxes, like little white logs, and the half-empty rolls of Certs. Did anybody imagine for one second that Becca Sawyer—Miss Straight A, Miss Goody-Goody, Miss Friends With All the Teachers—was planning to bring in an automatic weapon and shoot up the school?

Becca turned around and looked at me. And it was so obvious that she was in such total hell that later, all through the rest of that day, I could still see her face, the misery and panic on it.

Finally the prison-camp matron gave in and said okay and let Becca jam all the embarrassing articles back into her backpack.

I held my breath when it was my turn, but

they waved me through. I made it through the metal detectors without them going off.

That first week after Pleasant Valley, we went from one assembly every month to an assembly every morning. Our homeroom teachers gave us new schedules, fresh from the computer. Everything was basically the same except that every class period had been cut by five or ten minutes to make room for the whole school to get together in the auditorium. It didn't seem like that much of a change, except that assembly was seriously boring. Well, at least it wasn't class. You didn't have to pay attention.

One morning Dr. Willner got up on stage—once again with Mr. Trent, who was now standing silently beside him—and outlined the details of the new Central High dress code. Already Dr. Willner looked different, as if he'd settled in. His motions were less jerky and stiff. In fact he practically moonwalked up and oozed all over the podium.

He said, "As many of you know, public schools across the country are experimenting with school uniforms as a way of dealing with everything from cliques to overconcern with the latest fashions to gang membership and violence."

Most of us didn't know any such thing! Was he saying that we were going to start wearing uniforms, that from now on, going to Central would be like going to Catholic school and wearing those ridiculous blazers?

"But because we here at Central value the individuality of our students, we have decided against uniforms"—some mild whistling and cheers greeted this—"and have instead drawn up a list of limits beyond which we have decided that it is counterproductive and even dangerous for our students to trespass."

Avery said, "Did you see how he did that? The guy is really slick. Everybody's so happy they're not going to have to wear uniforms that some incredibly strict dress code will seem cool, by comparison."

Brian said, "Dude, I am *impressed*. The guy is a total genius."

This time, we were all sitting at the back of the auditorium, at least as far back as the juniors and seniors would let us get. But it seemed to us that Dr. Willner heard us whisper, and stopped a moment, and sought us out of the crowd.

"He's got our seats bugged," Silas said.

I said, "Silas, man, you've got to relax. This paranoia thing is catching. I mean, it's like you've got a cold and you're sneezing all over us."

"From now on," said Dr. Willner, "there will be no wearing of baseball caps backward."

All right. We'd expected that. Actually, Central had been a little behind the curve in lettings kids still get away with wearing baseball caps. Most schools had outlawed them years ago. We'd been lucky that Mr. Trent never noticed *what* we were wearing.

"And no more hats at all unless the temperature is below forty."

What about the skaters? What about that poor chemo kid in ninth grade? We needed a moment to think about it.

"No baggy pants. No bare midriffs."

Somebody whistled. Dr. Willner stopped and said, "I trust the faculty is making notes on those students who apparently feel compelled to express their opinions on a subject about which no opinions are needed. Impulse control is a subject we will take up in a future assembly. Now can we get back to business—to the business before us this morning?"

This was greeted by a smattering of applause. Dr. Willner smiled. What did he have to smile about? It wasn't that anyone agreed with what he was saying. It was just that some people—and I didn't blame them—would do practically anything to get this assembly over with and move on.

"No flip-flops. No sunglasses. No chains. No studded accessories. Though I cannot imagine that Central students would wear such items in the first place."

Did he not *notice* the row of goth kids, halfway back on the right? Was tongue piercing still okay? He didn't seem to have thought of that.

"No coats or jackets below the knees." We knew what *that* was about. The killers at Pleasant Valley had worn ankle-length trench coats. They were so unoriginal they couldn't even think of some new style that the kids at Columbine hadn't already tried.

"And finally, though I promise you that this will only be temporary, we have proposed a brief ban on wearing the color red."

Red? You could hear kids all over the auditorium saying the word. Red? We weren't allowed to wear *red*? It wasn't *my* favorite color, but still it seemed like a strange concept to remove an entire color from the available spectrum of what we could and couldn't wear.

"By which we mean *anything* red—solids, prints, accessories. As you may know, red is a common gang color. And more importantly for our purposes here, red kerchiefs and ribbons and ties were used by the killers at Pleasant Valley to exchange secret signals."

Suddenly I thought about Stephanie Tyrone, the eleventh grader who had worn a red ribbon every day since her older brother died of AIDS. Was Dr. Willner saying she couldn't do *that*? Practically all the guys in school had a crush on Stephanie, because she was really beautiful and popular and brave—and had had this romantic and tragic life. She'd mostly nursed her brother herself after he came home from San Francisco. I used to have fantasies in which I talked to her about my mom and asked her how come she didn't mind everyone knowing about her brother when I didn't like anyone, not even my friends, ever mentioning Mom. It wasn't a big secret or any-thing. I mean, my friends all knew about it when my mom died. I just never talked about it—though sometimes I wished I could have.

"As of now," Dr. Willner was saying, "that

includes all red badges, ribbons, and membership pins. Students will still be permitted to wear pins and images of the American flag, which, as you know, I *hope* you know, has red stripes." He waited. No one laughed. "All right, that's enough for the moment. We're cutting into valuable class time. Your homeroom teachers will give you copies of the new dress code. We hope you will take them home and familiarize yourself with the conditions and requirements. Any infringements of the code will automatically result in a two-day suspension."

By this point we were ready to agree to anything just to get out of that auditorium. Did he want us to come to school naked? Fine! Just don't make us sit here and listen anymore. Even first-period English was starting to seem appealing. By the time I finally stood up, both my feet were asleep, so I fell behind the other guys.

Eventually I found myself limping along next to Becca Sawyer.

She said, "This couldn't be worse."

tremors all the way back to the end of the line. Suddenly the door swung open, and Stephanie Tyrone sailed out. We hardly even had to look. We knew what had happened: She was still wearing her red ribbon. She'd never looked so pretty as she did then, holding her head up high, not focusing on anyone in particular as she ran down the stairs. You could practically feel a clean wind coming off her as she hurried past.

I wondered what she would do when her two-day suspension was over. Would she be willing to give up, roll over, and surrender? Or would she return with her red ribbon and get thrown out

"Which part?" I asked. I was mainly trying not to stumble and fall. One foot was still numb.

"The red part," she said. "I just bought this cool red sweater. I mean, with my own allowance."

That evening everyone was e-mailing back and forth, complaining about the new dress code and trying to figure out if there was anything we could do about it. Becca Sawyer sent out a group e-mail about the Danish resistance during the Second World War, how the Nazis ordered all the Danish Jews to wear a yellow star, and how the Danish king started wearing one, and then everybody else did, until finally the Nazis gave up trying to set the Jews apart.

Well, sure, I thought. I know what's on Becca's mind. She's upset about that new red sweater.

Someone said we should *all* wear red, and everybody said that was a great idea, they would do it. But then Avery wrote that no one was really willing to get into that much trouble just to wear red. Because they wouldn't suspend *everyone*, they'd just pick out a couple of us. He said everyone would promise to do it, but actually no one would. We all knew that Avery was right, as usual, so we gave up on that particular plan.

Silas sent out a message asking if everybody knew that during the 1950s, Communists were called Reds, and everybody hated them. Silas's e-mail had a P.S. Did anybody want to buy two slightly used marijuana-leaf T-shirts and another cool shirt with a picture of Bob Marley getting loaded?

I felt a little uneasy about it all. I mean, I resented the dress code as much as anyone else, but they hadn't banned anything that I would wear anyway. The year before in the ninth grade, I used to like to wear raggedy clothes. Whenever I got a new pair of jeans, I'd shred the bottoms with my mom's old cuticle scissors. But over the summer it struck me that it was totally fake to dress like a poor kid when I wasn't one. Not that we had

a lot of money. Illustrators like my dad exactly make a fortune, and we'd gotten poorer without the money my mom made ing English at UMass Amherst. That's where been going on the day she got killed. My dad I always made fun of her because the drive should have taken forty minutes took her alm two hours. I guess we never really understood till it was too late—how bad a driver she was.

Anyway, I couldn't imagine even wearing th stuff they'd outlawed: studded collars, baseba hats, chains, trench coats. Though now tha they'd forbidden all that, I almost wanted to dig old baseball cap fr

FOR THE NEXT FEW DAYS, there were no more new rules. We still had daily assembly, but now they were mostly lectures from Dr. Willner, general talks about building community spirit and preventing school violence. He'd stand up on stage with these pie charts and overhead projections and drone on and on about the importance of providing information and suggesting reading lists and holding workshops for students who felt depressed and alienated and angry about the crisis—the crisis we still hadn't had.

The rules were annoying, but still I wouldn't have called it a crisis. I still believed, I *wanted* to believe that Avery was right, that things would begin to ease up now, and that the worst part was over.

One morning the buzzer that signaled class changes and that called us to assembly began to sound, over and over, way louder than normal, as if whoever was pushing the button was in a red-hot rage. By the time we got to the auditorium, Dr. Willner was on stage, and it was clear from the look on his face that he was the button pusher. As usual, Mr. Trent stood beside him, looking even more out of it than usual, as if his brain were on vacation, or as if he'd just remembered something important that he'd left at home.

Even as we were taking our seats, we could see that Dr. Willner was holding up something—some dark object we couldn't identify from a distance. So that even those of us who usually made a point of sitting in the back rows moved toward the front so we could see what it was.

What he had was a piece of slime, a truly disgusting object that looked like a strip of that seaweed they serve in Japanese restaurants, only more gluey and soft.

Dr. Willner said, "I'm sure that most of you will not know what this is."

It was hard not to snicker, because of course no one had the slightest *idea* what it could be.

"Most of you, I am confident, go through your entire four years at Central without finding out about the dangers of objects like the one I am holding. But there are a few of you out there who are perfectly aware that this—this grotesque *thing*—is a marijuana cigarette."

Again it took major self-control not to crack up laughing. The most hard-core stoner would have had trouble figuring out that Dr. Willner's slime trail used to be a joint.

"This . . . repulsive *thing* was found in the bushes in front of the school."

My friends and I stopped laughing. This was highly unfortunate. This was downright bad. How could they have found it? Had someone seen Silas toss it in the bushes as we waited in line to get in? No wonder the joint looked so gross—that was days ago! We couldn't look at Silas, we didn't want to know what he was going through.

Or maybe they didn't see him throw it away, and somehow they just . . . found it. Maybe the guards who spent their days shaking down everyone coming into school spent their evenings going over the building and the grounds with a magnifying glass and tweezers.

"Dogs," whispered Silas. "It's got to be dogs. At night after everyone's gone home they bring in those pot-sniffing dogs, the K-9 crew working the night shift after their day jobs at the airport."

"As a consequence of this disturbing discovery," Dr. Willner was saying, "the school board has approved requiring random drug testing for participation in extracurricular school activities. Students wishing to take part in orchestra, chorus, newspaper, and team sports must agree to undergo random urine testing."

We didn't have a school newspaper! That's how much Dr. Willner knew. Only then did it hit us that he'd said team sports.

Brian whispered to Silas, "Thanks, man."

Silas said, "Brian, man, hey, shut up."

So things began to move quickly again. That same afternoon, after school, in gym, just before basketball practice started, Coach Petrocelli said, "Guys, come on. Can I have your attention? There's something I need to read you."

Everyone looked at everyone else. This wasn't going to be pleasant.

He read aloud from a photocopy. He didn't look up once.

"'In light of the recent tragedy at Pleasant Valley, and of our own Zero Tolerance policy, team members should be warned that team membership is contingent on passing random urine drug tests.'"

Brian said, "Are you *serious*?"

"I'm afraid so," said Coach Pete.

"What about our *rights*?" said Avery.

Coach Pete rolled his eyes.

Well, it was bound to happen, sooner or later. It was only a matter of time. I mean, we all knew that stuff like that had been going on for years, in other schools, in other parts of the country. Every so often you saw something about it on the news, or one of those TV newsmagazine shows my dad and Clara liked to watch.

Of course, we knew that it happened. But that was in *other* schools, closer to Columbine and Paducah. Which naturally explained everything. We were close to Pleasant Valley.

"Did you say *urine*?" Silas said. And everybody laughed.

Coach Pete said, "Silas, please. I don't know what to tell you guys. You know this isn't my idea. You know I don't need this." And it was true, we knew he didn't. Coach Pete had an autistic teenage daughter at an expensive residential school somewhere in Connecticut. Coach's wife, Anita, worked as a secretary in the front office. Knowing those things made us like and respect

Coach Pete even more—the fact that he had such a difficult home life and still could invest his whole heart and soul into whether or not the second-string team won or lost a basketball game. It made us play harder, it made us take the game seriously—as seriously as Coach Pete did.

"Plus I've got to *monitor* these . . . tests," he said. "Can you guys *believe* it? I've got to stand outside and listen while you guys whiz in a paper cup."

Just that word monitor gave me the creeps. But it took me a second to figure out why. Then I knew: It reminded me of that first e-mail my dad got from the school, advising parents to monitor their kids for anxiety and depression. We hadn't been anxious and depressed then. But now I could see where it could happen—coming to gym and never knowing if our urine was going to be tested could definitely be depressing.

"Gross," said Silas. "Man. That is *disgusting*." No one needed to be told that Silas was the Smart Jock most likely to fail the random drug test.

Everyone groaned and said how nasty it was and that they couldn't believe it.

"Now here's the bad news, guys," said Coach Pete. "We're starting today. I'm supposed to pick someone at random, but actually I think it would be better if I asked for a volunteer."

Silas, Avery, and Brian all looked at me, and then the rest of the team did, too. It just so happened that I didn't smoke weed. It wasn't as if I had a moral thing against it. But the only time I'd gotten high—this was at some ninth-grade party—I started thinking that all my friends hated me and that everybody was laughing at me. And then I started missing my mom almost more than I could stand. All it took was a few hits and I was twice as paranoid as Silas, which made me wonder why he smoked so much. So I hadn't exactly been eager to do that to myself again, though Silas kept saying that I should keep trying and shouldn't judge it from the first time. He'd said it was an acquired taste, like coffee and beer and olives.

"You hate beer," I'd reminded him.

"So far," Silas had agreed. "It's a taste I have yet to acquire."

Now you would have thought that the entire basketball team had suddenly developed an overwhelming fascination with their sneakers. Everyone stared at the floor. Because everyone knew that it was up to the Smart Jocks to find a way to protect Silas. It was our responsibility, and we accepted that, especially since we knew what the others didn't—namely that it was Silas who had pitched the joint into the bushes in the first place.

Obviously I was the one who ran the least risk of producing bodily fluids containing any detectable anything. I didn't even smoke cigarettes. Brian and Avery didn't smoke nearly as much weed as Silas, but they did sometimes, at parties on weekends. And our minds went blank as we tried to remember when the last party like that was.

At first I played dumb and tried to look as if I didn't know what anyone was thinking. I couldn't believe they'd be doing this to me, offering me up like some sort of sacrificial victim. Making me the team guinea pig for the first random drug test.

But as I looked around at my friends, I thought how guilty I'd feel if one of them got busted and thrown off the team. So I said, "Sure, great, why not? Let's do it."

The others actually applauded, the entire team. They were so relieved that they hadn't been chosen.

"Let's get it over with," said Coach. I guess he was being thoughtful, doing it right away so I wouldn't have to suffer in hell throughout the entire practice. To say nothing of how bad it would be for the whole team's concentration.

We stopped at Coach's office and got a paper cup from his desk and then headed through the showers to the bathroom. Under the circumstances, I decided to go into a stall, rather than use the urinal. As I went in, I watched Coach getting as far away from me as it was possible to be and still be in the same bathroom. He went over to the sinks and pretended to look at something in the mirror, some ingrown hair or troublesome zit that required his undivided attention.

They'd removed the locks from the stall doors. Since Pleasant Valley, I guess. I hadn't noticed before. It took me forever just to shut the door, holding the cup in one hand. Unzipping my zipper was another problem entirely. I don't know why it didn't occur to me to put the cup down on the floor.

I held the cup in front of me. Minutes passed. I couldn't do a thing. It was hideously embarrassing. I thought, We might have to be here all day. Or worse, we'd spend the entire practice like that, with me trying to whiz in the cup and Coach Pete waiting outside.

I tried to relax. I couldn't relax. I tried thinking of oceans, waterfalls. I couldn't think of a single water-based natural phenomenon that would make this any easier.

But sooner or later, somehow, something worked. Finally, I managed to fill the cup.

Carefully, *very* carefully, I put it down on the floor and zipped up my fly and opened the stall and went out and turned back and knelt and got the cup.

Coach Pete had a little white cardboard stick, which he dipped in the cup. He gave me a strained, pathetic smile. We couldn't have been more embarrassed.

"This is not supposed to change color," he said. "Let's hope it doesn't."

"Trust me. It won't," I said. I told myself I had nothing to worry about. But of course I was worried. One of things they'd talked about on the TV show that my dad and Clara watched were the kids who'd gotten nailed by false-positive results. It was like everything else that had happened since Pleasant Valley. Your punishment had nothing to do with whether or not you'd personally done anything wrong.

I held my breath. Coach Pete did, too.

The stick stayed white.

"Well, that's a relief," Coach Pete said. "I guess

the system works." And he checked my name off on a chart he'd brought with him.

Then we went back to practice, both of us so guilty and ashamed and red in the face it was almost as if we'd gone off together and had sex or something.

That night my dad and I and Clara went out for dinner at the diner on Route 7. Clara ordered the large Greek salad. I always thought it was funny that she was vegetarian. After all, she worked at Green Land, the local nursery, nurturing and tenderly growing all the little green things that she then turned around and gobbled up. Logically she should have been a carnivore, since she didn't actually work with—she didn't get so close to—actual living animals. A couple of times I almost mentioned this to my dad. But of course I didn't. First because it wasn't really logical at all; it sounded like Silas stoner logic. And second because it might have seemed like I was just finding reasons to criticize Clara, to imply that she was dorky. Which, I guess, I was.

Even though we made fun of people who talked about caring and sharing and getting in touch with your emotions, my dad and I were seriously conscious and thoughtful around each other—careful not to hurt the other person's feelings. Maybe it would have been different if he and my mom were divorced. Maybe then I could have thrown childish tantrums and said things like, "Clara isn't my mom!" But because my mom was dead, I felt I had to watch out for my dad. I *liked* him being with Clara. It took a lot of weight off me, and I was grateful for anything, for anyone who made him happy, or at least happier than he had been right after my mom died.

Anyway, Clara was nice enough. She tried to be friendly, always asking me about school. But it was hard to talk to her, and I just didn't see the point. She was pretty and younger than my dad. Frankly I sometimes found her irritating. She played the nature-girl thing pretty hard. Overalls. Straw in her long curly blond hair. Sometimes there was mud on her shoes and dirt under her fingernails.

Without our having to discuss it, my dad and I both knew that it was a night for the meat loaf special with mashed potatoes and gravy. Nell, our favorite waitress, figured it out right away. She brought me mashed potatoes on the plate and an extra side of mashed potatoes.

Nell said, "Honey, there are just some days when you can't get enough mashed potatoes."

We gave the meal our full concentration. No one said anything for quite a while. Once I lifted my head long enough to watch Clara tear into her salad. All those greens to chew, those carrot rounds to spear, those olive pits to spit out. It looked like a lot of hard work, more than it was worth. You burned more calories than you took in. No wonder Clara was so thin.

Finally Clara said, "So, Tom, how's school?"

Ordinarily I would have said, "Fine." In a tone

that made it clear: end of conversation. But seeing as how she'd asked, this was as good a time as any to give her and my dad some idea of what was happening.

"Really, really weird," I said.

"Weird how?" said my dad.

"Well, for one thing, ever since Pleasant Valley, they keep coming up with these long lists of new rules and requirements."

"Oh, like what?" said Clara. My dad was hardly listening. Maybe he already knew. I knew that the school had started e-mailing him nightly, to make sure that he had the new dress code and all the new regulations on his hard drive.

"Like random drug testing. Today I had to piss in a cup and Coach Pete tested it for cannabis."

"You had to *what*? The coach did *what*?" My dad put down his fork.

"Random urine testing," Clara said. "They make the kids urinate in a cup. Gosh. I knew that stuff happened but—"

Dad shook his head. "That's terrible," he said. But he didn't sound like he meant it. Maybe he thought that having to piss in a cup wasn't the most terrible thing in the world. When you actually thought about it, lots of things were worse—for example, what had happened at Pleasant Valley. Even so, I wanted the changes to stop. I wanted things to be the way they were before.

I said, "It's not just terrible, it's *really* terrible. Isn't it, like, against the law? Isn't there something you could do? I mean, a lot of parents would probably object, and you could all get together and talk to Mr. Trent—"

It occurred to me that Mr. Trent had been keeping a lower and lower profile since Dr. Willner had come to the school. Mr. Trent still stood up on stage with Dr. Willner every morning, but in terms of authority—of his being a presence at Central—you could say that Mr. Trent had basically left the building. We never heard his voice anymore on the PA system, only Dr. Willner's. It was almost as if there had been a peaceful coup, some kind of government takeover.

"And then what do we do?" said my dad. "Have meetings? Form a committee? Take it to the school board and get told to mind our own business? Or maybe bring it all the way to the Supreme Court, hire expensive lawyers and invest tons of money and time? And then have the Supreme Court remind us that drug testing has already been upheld in courts all over the country, that they themselves upheld it? It's the wave of the future, I'm afraid. Whether we like it or not. No one thinks kids deserve any rights anymore—certainly not since Columbine. There's nothing to do but put up with it. My sense is, it won't last. Pleasant Valley will be history, and they'll budget this out of existence."

It made it me feel slightly better that my dad wasn't more alarmed. And that he agreed with Avery—that the whole thing would blow over. At the same time I was disappointed that he wasn't offering to swing into action. I guess the bottom line was: Dad wasn't the one who had to whiz in a cup while Coach Pete waited outside. Let *him* try it a couple of times if he thought it wasn't so terrible.

"We could at least complain," Clara said. "Lodge a formal protest. Let them know that parents are watching and paying attention, and they're not happy about their kids' privacy being violated like that—"

My dad and I stopped and looked at her. She was usually very sensitive about not interfering, not saying anything about what happened between my dad and me. Actually, I sort of liked it now that Clara was on my side. But I didn't like her speaking for the "parents." Clara wasn't my parent and I didn't want her to forget that. I knew it was immature, but somehow it seemed more important for Clara to remember that she wasn't my mom than for her and my dad to save me from being randomly drug tested.

Then everybody fell silent, and it was one of those moments that happens with people you know well: Everyone knew what everyone else was thinking without anyone having to say it. Which was fine with me. How could I have explained what I had been thinking without totally blowing Clara away and ruining my dad's whole evening?

"Never mind, that's okay," I said. "You guys don't have to worry about it. I'm sure you're right. It's not really such a huge problem. And everything will calm down and get back to normal in a week or two."

"Take it easy, hang on till then," said Dad, returning to his meat loaf.

That night, after I'd gone to bed, Dad knocked on my door. "Tomster, can I come in? Are you asleep?"

In fact, I'd just been lying there, rigid and totally wired. I hadn't even been sleepy, but now I switched off the lights and grunted, "Yeah. Okay. Come in." For some reason, I wanted him to feel guilty about having woken me up.

"Can I turn on the light?" asked my dad.

"Sure," I said. "Go ahead. What's going on?"

"I wanted to apologize," he said.

"For what?" I said. "You didn't do anything wrong."

"Back in the diner . . ." he said. "I don't know. I don't want you to think that I wasn't paying attention, that I wasn't listening to you about the drug testing and the metal detectors and all the new rules at school. I realize it's a drag. But . . ." Just then, I noticed that he was holding a thick stack of papers that he handed to me.

"What the hell?" I said. But as soon as I looked at them, I could see what they were. He'd printed out all the e-mails he'd gotten from school since Pleasant Valley. I couldn't make much sense of them. Maybe I was sleepier than I'd thought. All I could make out were lots of charts and statistics, tables labeled SCHOOL KILLINGS SINCE 1995, and graphs with lines that rose and spiked and kept rising.

"It's worrisome," he said. "I guess I didn't know—I didn't *want* to know—how bad things were until the school started sending out this information. And when it happened so close to home, right here in Pleasant Valley—"

"Pleasant Valley isn't *here*," I said. "No one seems to get that part."

"It's close enough," said my dad. "Too close. And maybe I'm going about this all wrong, but I *want* you to be safe. I want you to be protected. And if the school is going a little overboard to make sure its students are safe, maybe that's not so bad. Ever since your mom died . . . I don't know, I realized I hadn't been careful enough. I mean, I'd made *fun* of her driving—"

"That's okay, Dad," I said. The truth was, at that moment—as coldhearted as it might seem—I would have said almost anything just to make him shut up. I didn't want to talk about my mom, or anyway, not then. It was strange. Right after she died, we used to talk about her a lot, but it had gotten harder and harder. And by now, it was sort of . . . embarrassing. As if her death were some awful secret that we shared and that made us different from other people. "Honestly, Dad, you don't have to explain. I know you're on my side."

"That's what I want you to know." He seemed relieved.

"I *do* know it," I said.

Dad kissed me on the forehead. "You're not too old for me to kiss good night?" he said.

"No," I said. I wasn't. And besides, he'd already kissed me.

"Well, then, good night. Love you," he said.

"Love you, too," I said.

After my dad left, I lay awake, thinking about all the things I wished I'd said to him. I *did* know that he wanted me to be safe and protected. But I was getting confused about what I needed protection *from*. Because so far, none of the backpack searches had turned up any guns or weapons. There was no evidence that anyone was plotting murder at Central.

On the other hand, it had been really humiliating, pissing in the cup for Coach Pete. At this point, I'd take my chances with the nonexistent psycho killers if we could just go back to the time when we could walk into school without waiting in line and wear anything we wanted and not have to think about what privileges we might lose tomorrow.

Why hadn't I said that to my dad? Because it wouldn't have helped. Because the truth was: What I really wanted was to tell my mom. Or, actually, to have her explain it to *me*, to straighten everything out, to help me figure out what to think, and for her to do what she did best: know what I was thinking without my having to say it.

What was strange about the teachers was how distracted and absentminded they seemed, as if they were always listening for something—some urgent new set of directions. Were they all doing what Dr. Willner said? What hold did he have on them? Almost all of them had tenure. In fact, everybody always complained about that because it meant even the worst teachers couldn't ever be fired, no matter how mean or incompetent they were. Even Mrs. Seidel, the geometry teacher, who used to water her plants in class and sprinkle the slow kids' heads and say she was watering the vegetables—even she had a contract guaranteeing her job until she decided to retire. So what did the teachers seem so worried about? Did they know something we didn't?

One day, in social studies, Mrs. Ridley said, "Is there anyone who would like to bring up a topic of general interest?"

The class was amazed to hear her ask the question she always used to ask. Because she'd basically stopped asking, ever since Pleasant Valley. Lately, we went straight to the day's lessons, without the discussions of stuff we'd seen in the paper and on TV. We were still on the Boston Tea Party, but nobody much cared or felt they had to pay attention. Because we'd done the Boston Tea Party practically every year since the fourth grade.

"Someone?" Then Mrs. Ridley caught herself, as if she were just as surprised as we were to hear the voice of her old self speaking.

Becca Sawyer said, "I have something I'd like to bring up. A lot of us feel strange about how different school's become. I mean, there's all this new stuff, like the metal detectors, the dress rules, and the random drug tests."

Becca sang in the chorus, and I suddenly wondered if she'd had to get tested, too. It would be even harder for girls. I didn't want to think about that.

Mrs. Ridley shook her head and frowned, and something went dead in her face. It was almost like *Invasion of the Body Snatchers* all over again. It was as if something snapped back in line, and Mrs. Ridley returned to her post–Pleasant Valley robotic self.

"What Central students need to understand," she said, "is that all of these new procedures are for their own good, their own safety and protection.

What if someone were allowed to bring a gun into school? What if someone came into this class with a concealed weapon? And what if a student came to school high on some dangerous drug and became violent and put the other students' lives at risk?"

"Then what are we protecting?" I said, surprising myself. "I mean, what's the point of going to school if it's like being sent to prison?" I reminded myself to remember this and say it to my dad the next time I found myself trying to explain my objection to all the new rules.

Mrs. Ridley stared at me. What I'd said wasn't computing for her. And for some reason, I got suddenly—and extremely—nervous. I'd been pulling down a B minus so far, mostly because Mrs. Ridley liked me. But it wasn't my grade I was worried about now. Whatever jitters I was feeling had nothing to do with that. Something else—something more serious—seemed to be going on here.

"Why . . . we're protecting human life. Keeping our community safe. *That's* the point," Mrs. Ridley explained in a patient, slightly singsong voice, as if she were teaching second graders.

"But no one's brought a gun to Central," said Avery.

"Not yet," said Mrs. Ridley.

"No. Not *ever*," said Brian.

"And no Central kid has ever flipped out on drugs," Avery added.

We all knew that Avery meant not in school. There had been that one famous party where a girl drank quarts of beer and took a tranquilizer, and they had to call her parents to come and get her and take her to the emergency room.

Mrs. Ridley smiled sweetly. "Brian. Avery," she said. "Let me remind you. This is not a court of law. This is a public high school."

"This is a concentration camp," Brian muttered softly, but loud enough for everyone to hear.

"It absolutely is not!" said Mrs. Ridley. "It is not only wrong but tasteless to compare your school—to which you are free to come and go as you please, and in which you are obliged to obey a few perfectly reasonable rules—to those vicious, evil camps where the Nazis murdered six million innocent Jews."

I had to admit she was right about that. I was sorry Brian said that. It was taking things too far. Also it was good to see Mrs. Ridley get so excited, even if she was angry. It sounded like her old self, her pre–Pleasant Valley self coming through. And for that one moment I was almost able to convince myself that she was still the same person and that maybe nothing had changed.

They must have had some plans already in place, because the changes happened so fast. One Friday afternoon the buses dropped us off at home. And by Monday morning the same buses picked us up—but now they all had TV. It was astonishing that they got it together so quickly, when everything else took so long. Big Dave, our bus driver, had been driving with a funky windshield-wiper blade since the start of the school year, and he had put in a dozen complaints, and the company still hadn't fixed it. The wiper still streaked the windshield, but now there was a TV set wedged up high under the roof, every fourth or fifth row.

When I got on the half-full bus, everyone was looking up and in the same direction, and it took me a while to realize what was going on. As always, I went to the back of the bus where Silas, Avery, and Brian had staked out the last two sets of seats. It was tenth-grade territory; we were the oldest, we claimed it. Most of the eleventh graders had their driver's licenses or else got rides from seniors.

For a minute I thought that the TV could be entertaining. Maybe they had cable and we could watch MTV. It would make the trip go faster and seem less boring.

"Wake up, dimwit," Brian said. "This is not *The Real World*."

I could hardly hear him, that's how loud the sound was. A deep male voice boomed out of the speakers. "Our brave forefathers . . . All the signers of the Declaration of Independence fought in the Revolutionary War . . ."

What had I been *thinking*? Of course it wasn't MTV. It was Bus TV. It was "Great Moments in History." I glanced up and watched three men in Revolutionary War uniforms signing the Declaration of Independence. It reminded me of those cheesy reenactments they staged on the Fourth of July in the city park in Lenox. I had a feeling that there was something wrong. It was like: What's wrong with this picture? But I lost interest long before I could figure out what it was.

"How intensely does this suck?" Brian said.

Avery said, "This is so pathetic."

"Come on, guys," said Silas. "You can sort of get into it. Those powdered wigs made them look like some '80s hair band. And I dig the crappy low-resolution screen, those little blobs of bad color." He was gazing at the TV screen, transfixed. It was only eight thirty in the morning, and poor Silas was totally gone. We were starting to worry about him, to wonder if maybe his smoking hadn't spiked in the last couple of weeks. One of the e-mails my dad got from school had warned parents to be on the watch for signs of increased drug use in the aftermath of events like Pleasant Valley. It bothered us that Silas might be proving them right.

The TV blared on and on. There was an endless close-up of a fake old document with some spidery writing on it. Frankly, I never imagined that there would be a day when I would be complaining about too much TV. But I guess that day had come.

I thought about all the ways in which school *was* getting to be like an airport. First the lines to get in the door. Already we had names for the guards: Fat Man. Bug Boy. Miss Prune. It was our small way of getting back at them for how exposed we felt as they pawed through our stuff. And for how much they seemed to *enjoy* it. And now we had TVs like the ones in the airport departure lounges, though even CNN would have been a million times better than "Great Moments in History." The point was that you couldn't *not* watch. You could hold out for a while, but finally you sank into it and let it take you over. First Avery and then Brian slid down in their seats and zoned out on the TV. Silas was already in the zone. He'd been there from the beginning.

I stared out the window at the rolling fields disappearing behind the bright patches of forest. Half the leaves had come down; they'd fallen early this year. There had been a big wind storm the night before. October was always my favorite month, but now it didn't make me happy.

I missed the bus *without* TV. I missed joking around with my friends and then taking a break from joking around and looking out the window. Having TV on the bus should have meant there were more choices, more things to do. But the TV took over, it controlled the whole bus, and nothing else could compete.

Again, I remembered that blues line: *You don't*

miss your water . . . That song used to run through my head all the time, right after my mom died, and now it kept coming back to me. I couldn't get it out of my mind. The way that Central used to be before Pleasant Valley was seeming more and more like some happy childhood dream that was lost and gone forever. Maybe Dr. Willner was right about our having grown up. We couldn't just be kids anymore. We were as sad as adults.

But of course we couldn't have known that what was about to happen would make that first day of Bus TV seem like another lost golden time.

four

T WAS JUST A FEW DAYS later that the guard we called Bug Boy decided to make a microscopic inspection of every millimeter of my backpack. I don't know exactly why we called him that; his eyes weren't buggy, exactly. I suppose he reminded us of something you'd find beneath a rock or crawling up the underside of a leaf. Also his hands were hairy and sort of sticky, so that when he dug them around in my backpack, I knew that something would come up stuck to them—in this case, a half-empty package of ChocoShake chewing gum.

"Not allowed," he said. "Verboten." He tossed the gum into this huge plastic trash bin the guards kept behind them. By ten o'clock in the morning it was always almost full, mostly with girl stuff—eyelash curlers, nail files—you couldn't bring into school anymore. Also, the rules kept changing, so it was tricky to keep track of what was allowed and what wasn't. You had to pay close attention. We were encouraged to ask our parents about the e-mails they got every night, detailing the new regulations.

Still, I seemed to have missed the part about chewing gum being illegal. You weren't supposed to chew it in class. But as far as I could tell, it was neither a drug nor a weapon. So there was no good reason why you couldn't bring it into school.

"Not allowed since *when*?" I said.

Bug Boy stopped and stared at me. Students never talked back to the guards. We'd found out, very early on, how much time that could add to your average morning inspection. When the guards said "not allowed," you rolled over and gave it up. Whatever *it* happened to be.

"Lookit," said Bug Boy. "Why take *my* word for it? Why not go take it up with Dr. Willner? We'll save the gum right here for you, and if he says it's okay . . . well, fine, you can have it back later."

Fat chance I was going to go and see Dr. Willner to discuss ChocoShake gum. I knew kids who had been called into his office. It wasn't a pleasant experience. They said Dr. Willner was completely demented. He would give you and your parents these warm sympathetic looks even while he was telling you that this would be your final warning before he totally ruined your life. So far no one had gone beyond the final-warning stage, so people must have believed him without him having to explain precisely how he planned to ruin it. From the beginning, he'd understood what every three-year-old knows: that the vague threat is way scarier than knowing how much trouble, exactly, you're facing.

What we wouldn't have given to be called into Mr. Trent's office and have him forget, in mid-conversation, why we were there! But there was no longer any such thing as being sent to see Mr. Trent. If you screwed up now, Dr. Willner was your man, the guy you had to deal with. And poor Mr. Trent could have been a human-sized cloth dummy propped up on stage beside Dr. Willner at morning assembly.

"That's okay, enjoy the gum," I told Bug Boy. Even as I said it, I had the strangest feeling, as if I'd briefly left my body and were watching myself from a distance, insulting Bug Boy, making my life a lot harder. From now on, I could count on a daily backpack search.

By the time I gathered my things and put them in my backpack, I was among the last to get into school. As I walked through the ground-floor hall, I could tell that something new had happened. There were little groups of kids clustered by the lockers, whispering. Everybody looked crazed.

I saw a guy from my math class. "Random locker searches," he said. "A couple of kids on every hall had their lockers searched last night."

"Did they find anything?" I asked.

"Probably," said the kid.

Though running in the halls had *never* been allowed, I ran up the hall, trying to visualize the inside of my locker. It was early enough in the semester so that it wasn't yet the overstuffed junk heap on which you could hardly close the door. It usually didn't get like that until after Christmas. But still I couldn't think what I had in it, or what might be forbidden. One of the new forbidden things was gum, and I hadn't even known *that*.

I was hardly breathing when I opened my locker door. All right! Fine! I exhaled. Everything looked normal; that is, everything was a mess. What could I have been worried about, considering what was here? Some socks, a pair of extra sneakers, a rain jacket my dad made me bring in, a couple of books and CDs, broken earphones from an old Walkman.

I was so relieved. I felt great. I started to close my locker, and then I spotted the notice taped to the inside of the locker door.

TO THE OWNER OF THIS LOCKER.

Just in case I wasn't sure who that owner might be, my name, "Tom Bishop," was written under it in Magic Marker. The rest of the notice was printed. I was politely requested and strongly encouraged to schedule a conversation with Dr. Willner about the contents of my locker.

The contents of my locker? They must have made a mistake. Meanwhile it was creepy to think that someone had been here and gone through my personal belongings. I checked the few CDs I had, some books. Nothing had been taken.

The rest of the notice informed me that unless I appeared in Dr. Willner's office by last period this afternoon, I'd be facing an automatic two-day suspension.

So really I had nothing to lose. I might as well get it over with. Let Dr. Willner smile and threaten me with my "last warning." Maybe he would even tell me what I was being warned about.

I had fourth and fifth periods free. Even if I had to wait to see Dr. Willner, I figured I could probably get in and out without missing class. I found Dr. Willner's office at the far end of the second-floor corridor, a part of the school where I hardly ever went. I couldn't remember what had been there before Dr. Willner came to the school.

There was a narrow vestibule where Dr. Willner's secretary sat at a desk, working on a computer. She looked familiar, and then it hit me that it was Anita, Coach Pete's wife. I'm pretty sure she recognized me, but she pretended not to.

"I'm Tom Bishop," I said. "Dr. Willner wanted to see me."

She found my name on a list and checked it off.

"There're three people ahead of you," she said. "It's two doors down on the right."

The door was closed, and on it a large sign said SAFE ROOM, though you wouldn't have thought so from the expressions on the faces of the kids waiting outside. Actually, I was a little surprised, because I thought there would be dozens of kids. The fact that there were only three of them made it seem more alarming. I wish I knew how many lockers they'd searched.

The little ninth grader in front of me looked petrified with fear. "Hey, dude," I said encouragingly. "What did they get *you* for?"

"I don't know," he said. "They went through my locker last night, but I don't know what they found."

I made a joint-sucking motion and raised my eyebrows.

"No, not me, never," he said.

"Sure," I said. "Tell it to the judge. We know all about you ninth graders."

It wasn't very mature of me, torturing a younger guy. But it made the time pass, it kept my mind off my own problems.

Finally the door swung open, and a kid came out.

Silas looked so totally freaked, so completely unlike himself, that it took me a little while just to figure out who he was.

"Silas, are you okay?" I said.

"Yeah," he said. "I'm fine. I've never been better."

"You don't look fine," I said.

"Things got a little hairy in there."

"Meaning what? How hairy?" I said.

But at that moment the door opened again, and Dr. Willner poked his head out. I wished he hadn't done that. And what I wished even more was that I didn't feel so weird about him seeing me with Silas. It was as if I didn't want Dr. Willner spotting me, talking to a kid who was clearly in so much trouble. Even if he was one of my best friends. I took a few steps away from Silas and turned slightly toward the wall as if I were checking out the decorations, the posters and art and stuff. Except that there weren't any posters or art—nothing except a dusty mirror in which I saw this red-faced, guilty-looking guy who happened to be me. I couldn't believe how awful I felt! I'd known Silas since the first grade! And just one look from Dr. Willner had turned me into such a chicken that I was practically pretending not to know him. Right then I made a promise to myself. Whatever happened, no matter what vague or specific punishment anyone threatened us with, I would stick by my friends.

The kid at the head of the line went in. I assumed that, while I awaited my turn, I'd hear what happened to Silas. But Silas gave me a squirrelly look and said, "See you, dude. I think I need to get home before my parents read their e-mail."

After that, I didn't feel much like chatting with the terrified ninth grader. I didn't even smile encouragingly at him when his turn finally came. I could tell from his face when he came out that it hadn't been so bad, and I thought, What am *I* so worried about? There was nothing in my locker. Hadn't Dr. Willner said that he wanted to schedule time to get to know us all, individually? Maybe that was all this was. An easy few minutes of meet and greet.

When I walked in, Dr. Willner was reading

something on his desk. It reminded me of going for my annual medical checkup. Dr. Gold had known me since I was a baby, but he still read my name off my chart as he walked into the freezing cold office where I sat on the table in the ridiculous paper robe. But what Dr. Willner was reading seemed to be a list, and when I said my name, he ran his finger down it and frowned and said, "Ah, yes, Bishop. It seems we have a problem."

"What kind of problem?" I hated it that my voice shook, even slightly.

"Nothing life threatening," he said, and for the first time he looked up and fixed me with his dark snaky eyes peering out from under his bushy Abraham Lincoln eyebrows. I understood what the other kids meant about his trick of making his face sympathetic and menacing at the same time. "But a sort of . . . early warning symptom, a sign . . . of something we might need to watch. To make sure that it doesn't become more of a problem further down the road. What is it that the doctors say?

Early detection, early cure."

I felt like he was telling me that I had cancer, and I nearly asked him—just to be funny—if that's what he was doing. I was glad I'd had that run-in with Bug Boy earlier that same morning. It had taught me a lesson; it had gotten that rebellious, back-talking impulse completely out of my system. So now I just bit the bullet and repeated, "What kind of problem?"

"Not a problem for us so much as a problem for *you*." Dr. Willner sounded almost cheerful. "That's who stands to be harmed here. It's not that we're suggesting that you're in any way a hazard to your fellow students. But rather that some simple mistakes might make you a danger to *yourself*."

"Mistakes like what?" I wasn't getting this. What was I missing here?

"Tim . . ." said Dr. Willner.

"That's *Tom*," I said.

It was then that he focused on me and made eye contact so heavy that just looking back at him felt like lifting weights. And it was then that I decided that Dr. Willner was all threat and meanness, and that the sympathy was just a cover, camouflage, a false impression he knew he needed to give. As he stared into my eyes, I knew, beyond any doubt, that Dr. Willner despised me, that his rage was deep and endless.

But how could he have hated me? He didn't even know me. He didn't know the rotten things about me, the fact that sometimes I liked Clara to feel bad about herself, and that I liked my dad to feel bad about Clara. And also that there were times when I sat back and let Brian and Avery pick on Silas until it bordered on being ugly. The thought of Silas made everything worse. Poor Silas, where was he now? What was happening to *him*? I wished I'd been nicer to him all along. Maybe he would never have become such a stoner in the first place.

But Dr. Willner didn't know how I laughed when Brian and Avery made fun of Silas's conspiracy theories until he got even more para-noid and almost started crying. Without knowing any of that, Dr. Willner hated me just the same. And suddenly I understood. It was enough, he hated me just because I was young, and he wasn't. Did it make it better or worse that it wasn't per-sonal? Better *and* worse. Better because it wasn't my fault, I didn't have to feel guilty. And worse because it couldn't be fixed or changed. I couldn't charm him into liking me. There was nothing I could do.

"Tom," he said. "Excuse me. I won't forget the next time."

A chill shot from my neck to the base of my spine. I didn't want there to be a next time.

"Tom, we've asked the community to pay very close attention to the lists of those things we think are helpful or, alternatively, harmful for our stu-dents. You *do* know, Tom, that students are advised to ask their parents to share their nightly e-mail so that all of us can keep abreast of the school's rapidly changing programs and ideas? Plus, of course, any new rules and restrictions that are generated by these discussions and forums. We've also asked the homeroom and the social studies teachers to keep their students informed of the latest changes."

We got the lists in homeroom, not in social studies. I wondered if Mrs. Ridley couldn't bring herself to do it. Dr. Willner put out such a mind-reading vibe that I felt as if just my *thinking* about that might get Mrs. Ridley in trouble.

"By the way, Tom, how are you doing? How are you adjusting to the unfortunate measures—the metal detectors, the backpack searches—that this current time of crisis makes so regrettably necessary?"

"Fine," I said. "I'm doing okay." He was forcing me to lie, and we both knew it. If I hadn't been a total coward, I would have begun by asking what the crisis *was*, exactly.

"Oh, good. I'm delighted to hear that." A distant look came into his eyes, as if he were following some lesson he'd learned in grief and crisis 101. "Really, what we want is for our students to heal and recover and function at the top of their form. So we've been taking the first in a series of long, hard looks at our curriculum and our culture. And there are a few corrections we're making, a few things we're discouraging students from including in their daily lives."

Was this all about the *gum*? Because if it was, I could just leave it at home. It wasn't a big deal. But it couldn't have been about the gum. The note was already in my locker before the gum incident happened.

"Tom," said Dr. Willner. I wished that he would stop saying my name. I wished I'd never corrected him, that I'd let him keep saying Tim. "Let's cut to the chase here. We found not one but two of those . . . questionable items in your locker during our random locker search."

Sneakers? Was it sneakers? No more sneakers? Or the rain jacket that my dad made me bring?

This still wasn't computing. Someone must have planted something. Who hated me enough to do that?

"One of them is a book," he said. "J. D. Salinger's *The Catcher in the Rye*."

But they read that in junior English! That's how I'd gotten it last spring, from a rising senior on the basketball team who was getting rid of all his books at the end of the school year. I was reading the book an entire year before I had to read it for school. I shouldn't be getting in trouble for this. I should be getting extra credit!

"After much debate, we have decided to remove *The Catcher in the Rye* from our literature curriculum. Studies have proved that it has a terribly deleterious—*destructive*—effect on students too young to realize that Holden Caulfield is a highly negative role model. His attitude is not one that we should ever allow ourselves to have, or even condone. *Approve of*."

I knew what deleterious and condone meant.

It was totally insulting that he thought he had to translate all the big words for an idiot like me.

"What we've noticed is how often Salinger's novel has turned up among the most cherished possessions of students with suicidal tendencies, students who attempted and even succeeded in killing themselves." Dr. Willner paused a moment to let this sink in. "A kind of overidentification seems to take place with Holden and his complaints, to the detriment of the students, who should be given more positive models of how young people their age should think and behave. They start to think they *are* Holden Caulfield—"

Wait a minute! Did Dr. Willner imagine that I believed I *was* Holden Caulfield? Or that I was anything like him? I never thought he was a role model, just a character in a novel! I liked being in Holden's brain, hearing his private thoughts. But my life was completely different from his. I had friends, I liked my dad. And I hadn't really hated school until after Pleasant Valley.

None of that had anything to do with how much I'd liked reading it. Or at least I *had* liked most of it. I quit about ten pages from the end. I don't know why I stopped. That was right after Pleasant Valley, right after everything changed. I kept thinking that if Holden Caulfield was whining so hard about things like adults being phonies, I'd like to see how he handled backpack searches and metal detectors. And though I knew it shouldn't have mattered—how was Salinger supposed to know what was going to happen to *us*?—it turned me against the book. I lost sympathy, somehow.

Even so, I didn't see why I shouldn't be able to read it if I wanted. I thought of my dad, at work at his desk, slaving away at his illustrations of beans. I imagined telling him about this. I pictured how steamed he would get. The whole subject of book banning made my dad start ranting and raving. He listened to NPR while he worked; that's where he heard about books being removed from school and library shelves.

The fact was, he'd been so happy when he'd found out I was reading *The Catcher in the Rye*. I didn't read that many books. Most of the time he worried that I watched too much TV. I hadn't had the heart to tell him I didn't finish the novel. And I knew it would make him furious to find out I'd gotten in trouble just for having it in my locker.

"State law, which we expect to change momentarily, still . . . regrettably . . . prohibits us from seizing cultural artifacts of this sort when we find them in a student's possession. So we are asking our students to agree voluntarily to the swift removal of all offensive articles from school property. And ideally they should arrange for their subsequent and complete disposal."

"Fine. I'll take it home. I'll lose it on the way home. I'll throw it in the trash. Whatever. But . . . you said that there were two things in my locker."

"Right." Dr. Willner checked his list. I wished I hadn't asked. Maybe he would have forgotten the second thing. "The other is a CD by a group called "T-u-f-f. K-n-o-x."

It took me a minute to follow the spelling. "You mean Tuff Knox?" I asked.

The name made Dr. Willner wrinkle his nose in disgust. Or maybe it was the bad spelling that made him so queasy. "Rap and hip-hop music is a whole category of adolescent culture that we have decided to discourage."

"But Tuff Knox are *girls*," I said, as if that explained everything. "It's not even real rap music. It's hip-hop for kids who don't really like hip-hop." Normally I never would have admitted that. I must have been desperate.

"Tom, this group is on a list that has been making the rounds of guidance and grief and crisis counselors like myself in schools all over the country. Music such as this leads to harder music, and no one needs to be reminded of the degree to which rap glorifies handgun use, the murder of innocent policemen, sex, and violence against women."

"Tuff Knox?" I couldn't bring myself to say that their songs were about their . . . boyfriends.

Dr. Willner took a deep breath and coughed.

"Tom, the ideal thing would be to have students trying to stay a little *ahead* of our plans for Central instead of a little *behind* the curve. As *you* have been, I'm afraid. Behind. The students we value most are the ones who can anticipate where all of this is going and who can get there before us."

I guess that counted me out. I really couldn't see where any of this was going, except toward some totally fascist system I didn't even want to imagine. Once more I thought of poor Silas, who had a pretty clear vision of the twisted, ugly road down which—if Dr. Willner got his way—we were directly headed. But I didn't think Dr. Willner was talking about students like Silas. What he meant by anticipate was to be completely with the program. Students who *anticipated* would be willing to do whatever it took to make sure that other kids—the rebels and slackers and stragglers—got with the program, too. I didn't want to imagine that, either. Suddenly, I felt exhausted. If I could only get out of that office and back to class, and then home, maybe then I could start to sort things out.

"Fine," I said. "Sure. Whatever." The first rule of teenage common sense. Don't make more trouble for yourself at the moment when you're about to be let off with a warning.

"Tom," said Dr. Willner. "I'm awfully glad that we've gotten this chance to get to know each other. And I do hope that before too long I will get a chance to meet your father, who, I understand, is an illustrator."

Man, I really hoped not. I didn't want to be there. There was no way a meeting between Dr. Willner and my dad could turn out to be anything I wanted to witness. I hated to think of my dad giving in, knuckling under to Dr. Willner, acting pretty much like I was acting right now. On the other hand, I didn't want him to go off on Dr. Willner and make a giant fuss, which I would definitely pay for. I'd be the one who'd get to eat it, every minute of every school day. The idea of my dad and Dr. Willner in the same room upset me so much that it took a while for me to be upset that he knew what my dad did for a living. At any rate, it made me think twice about rushing home to announce to my dad that I'd been told I couldn't read *The Catcher in the Rye*. That would definitely be the spark that set off the major battle. And I wasn't sure I was ready to see—or to *be*—the collateral damage.

"Sure, that would be great," I said. "You and my dad would like each other." And only after I'd lied that much did Dr. Willner let me go.

"*Liking* is not the point," he said, but he had gone back to looking at his list. He was already finished with me. He'd moved on to a new case, to the next kid who needed his help.

A book, a CD. Whatever. I thought I'd gotten off easily, nothing too serious had happened, except that I'd found out, more or less for a fact, that Dr. Willner hated me. Still, I didn't feel nearly as bad as

Silas looked on his way out of Willner's office.

I went directly to the lunchroom to see if I could find Silas.

Of my friends, only Brian was there, talking to some hot girl in tight jeans and a low-cut sweater.

"Andrea, this is Tom," said Brian.

"Nice to meet you." It was obvious that Andrea was just being polite and was wishing I'd disappear so she could go back to being alone with Brian.

I asked Brian if he'd seen Silas. He said no, he hadn't, not for a while. I said I'd seen Silas leaving Dr. Willner's office looking totally fried.

Brian said, "Combined with the locker search, that is not great news, my friend."

"Poor guy," said Andrea, but it was just for Brian's benefit, and both of us ignored her.

We assumed we'd see Silas at practice. But Silas wasn't there. Coach Pete told us that Silas had gone home sick in the early afternoon. I thought about Coach Pete's wife, working in Dr. Willner's office. I wondered how much she knew. All day I'd been thinking about *Invasion of the Body Snatchers*, about how certain people knew the truth about what was happening and tried to alert the world and then got turned into alien pods—and silenced forever.

Silas's absence turned out to be the least of Coach Pete's problems. Coach stood in front of us, wringing his hands, in that way we'd learned to recognize. It meant that he had some fresh nightmare to announce. Poor Coach Pete! He was such a laid-back, good-hearted guy. Everybody liked him. He wasn't one of those coaches who pretended they were a honcho marine in some boot-camp training exercise, or the kind who tortured you just because they had the power. Like Coach Stevens, the soccer coach, who made his team run around the field five times on the coldest days and at the very end of the longest, most exhausting practices.

We all knew that Coach Pete hadn't signed on to be our prison guard or to be a cop, to dip little wooden wands in our bodily fluids and to get us into trouble. So we all felt sorry for him and tried to cooperate, and to make whatever he had to do as easy as possible.

Now he said, "It's been brought to the administration's attention that I've been letting you guys on the basketball team volunteer for the drug tests."

Who brought that to their attention? I knew what Silas would have said: They've got the whole school bugged. Silas was definitely ahead of the curve, though not in the way Dr. Willner meant. Coach Pete said that it was the school's opinion that letting kids volunteer defeated the entire purpose of the random drug test.

"Guys, you gotta admit they're right . . . So . . . gee . . . uh . . . as much as I hate to . . . Brian, how about you, man? You think we can do this today?"

I tried to remember what day of the week it was, and what we'd done over the weekend, and if there had been a party, and if Brian had gotten high. I could see that Brian was trying to remember the same things. But Brian always thought faster than me, and the confident look that came over his face was supremely reassuring.

"Let's do it," Brian said.

Coach and Brian took off in the direction of the boys' bathroom. The Dumb Jocks did some layups and hoop shots, but nobody's heart was in it. It seemed like years till Brian and Coach Pete returned.

As soon as Brian saw me and Avery, he grinned and put up his thumbs. I was glad not to have two of my friends taken out on the same day. It was such a huge relief, considering how worried I'd been when they were in the bathroom. You would have thought that they were in there playing Russian roulette, and that we'd all been hanging around outside, waiting to hear the shot.

five

ILAS DIDN'T ANSWER his phone or respond to his e-mail. That night Brian, Avery, and I left him about ten messages apiece. After that we just started calling and hanging up on his machine.

The next morning he wasn't on the bus. We were all too dejected to talk. We just sat there watching "Great Moments in History," an episode about the Wright brothers that ended with a long speech about why the secret of flight could never have been discovered anywhere but in North Carolina. It was something about the air currents, and the temperature, and pure homegrown American ingenuity and genius.

Avery said, "This is pure propaganda. Can you guys believe this? Why exactly did it have to be an American? If some crackers down in North

Carolina hadn't figured it out, sooner or later some Frenchman or some Englishman or some African dude would have gotten it together. Man, haven't they ever heard of Leonardo da Vinci? The guy was practically *there*. He invented a flying machine. And dude, he was an *Italian*."

I felt so miserable about Silas that I briefly considered going down to the nurse and faking a stomachache painful enough to get myself sent home. Then, just as we were getting off the bus, Brian said, "Look at that."

There was Silas waiting in line to get into school with his parents. I'd never been so happy to see anyone in my life. Though I never would have admitted it, not even to Brian and Avery, the truth was I'd started thinking that maybe Silas had just vanished into thin air, like Stephanie Tyrone.

We realized that this was probably not the ideal moment to go over and bump shoulders with Silas and say, "Hey, man, good to see you." He and his mother and father seemed cut off from the rest of the world, floating up the stairs and into the school in their own private bubble of dread. Silas's mom had been friends with my mom. They both taught at the college. Mostly Silas's mom gave mine a ride to work. But she'd had the semester off when my mom got killed.

Seeing her reminded me of how my mom used to dress, her slightly baggy suits and long skirts: female college professors trying to be professional and stylish. Like my mom, she wore her hair shoulder length, wavy. Flyaway. But unlike Silas's mother, my mom was really pretty. Whenever I met the people she taught with, I could sense that the male teachers liked her, that they even had crushes on her, and I sort of liked it.

Anyway, I was glad that *my* mom wasn't being forced to stand there and stare at the ceiling while the guard we called Miss Prune emptied out her purse, which contained more junk than any normal kid's backpack. Silas's dad looked as if he couldn't decide whether to kill someone or burst into tears. I had the impression that Silas was about to throw up, but I couldn't tell whether it was because his mom was being practically strip-searched in front of the whole school, or because of the reason they were there in the first place. A friendly chat with Dr. Willner, no doubt. How thoughtful of the administration to schedule their visit so Silas and his parents would have to arrive along with the entire student body and couldn't sneak in quietly, on the sly, after classes started.

Silas's mom's purse was still getting the going-over when I slipped past him on the other line. I punched his arm and said, "Later." I wondered if I should have wished him good luck, if that would have made him feel better or worse.

In fact Silas and his parents *could* have come in later. They must have had to wait while Dr. Willner addressed the morning assembly. He told us that the state was considering raising the minimum driving age to eighteen. How the legislature voted would depend on the feedback it received from high schools all over the state, including Central. So we could safely assume that the final decision on the driving age would have something to do with how well or badly Central students behaved.

No one could believe it. This was the worst thing ever. You got your license at seventeen. Everybody did. It was like eating and breathing and sleeping—an essential human activity, a necessity of life. A basic right. It meant *freedom*.

"Driving is a privilege. Not a right," Dr. Willner informed the school as if he'd read our minds. The idea of having to go another year without driving, without being able to have our own lives, without being able to go to the mall or anywhere without being dragged around by our parents—the prospect seemed so grim that I briefly forgot about Silas.

He showed up in social studies. When Brian, Avery, and I saw him, we all pumped our fists in the air. Then we had to get back to what we were doing, which was writing paragraphs and correcting one another's work. Mrs. Ridley went around the room, pairing us up in groups of two, and by the time she got through, I was working with Becca Sawyer.

"Just write without thinking," Mrs. Ridley said as she often did. No one ever asked why we did this English-class-type exercise in social studies. Maybe it was because we hardly did anything in English class. We just read pointless stories aloud from the reader and answered the even more pointless questions that followed at the end of the stories.

I couldn't think of anything to write, so I scribbled a few sentences about how you never knew how much you cared about something till it was gone and then you really missed it. I suppose what got me started was Silas coming back, but I guess I was also talking about my mom and about the way school used to be before Pleasant Valley.

Becca worked on hers longer than I worked on mine. That wasn't exactly a surprise. She always wrote twice as much as anyone else. But fine, it gave me some downtime, a couple of minutes to kill. I put down my pen and spaced out and watched the morning sunlight shining through Becca's yellow hair.

Finally I gave her my paper. She read through it quickly.

"That's really beautiful," she said softly. I hated and loved the sympathy that kept welling up in her eyes.

I took her paper and began to read about how she was seriously spooked because it seemed to her that Central High was turning into a police state. But what spooked *me* was when she wrote how especially cruel it was to search teenagers' backpacks and subject kids to random drug testing when everyone knew that teenagers were the most easily embarrassed and self-conscious human beings in the world. The strange thing was that I'd thought that, just a few days ago. It freaked me out, but I liked it that Becca and I were thinking the same way. Because, for one thing, everyone knew she was really smart.

Becca's paper was perfect, obviously. I kind of whispered, "I know what you mean." That was pretty much all I could say. There were no corrections to make. She made a few light marks on mine, smiling apologetically over every tiny change. Then we waited for Mrs. Ridley to come around and check us.

Mrs. Ridley read mine and nodded, hardly looking at me. But after she read Becca's she stopped, and glanced up, and said, "Becca, you know . . . I don't think you should keep this in your folder."

We were each supposed to keep a folder in which we put everything we wrote during the term. We'd hand it in at the semester's end and, according to some mysterious formula, it would figure into our grade.

"Maybe you should take it home." Mrs. Ridley looked worried.

Becca was confused. "Do my parents need to sign it?" Mrs. Ridley made us do that sometimes, when we'd written an especially careless, sloppy, or lazy paper. That had never happened to Becca. That would have been a real first.

"Take it home and destroy it," Mrs. Ridley said.

That Saturday Silas, Avery, Brian, and I hooked up at the mall. My dad didn't like me hanging out there, so I had to remind him that it wasn't my idea to leave Boston—where he and my mom had met and where they lived before I was born—and move out here to the boondocks, where it was either the mall or nowhere. Sometimes when I was in an especially terrible mood, I'd tell my dad that I wished they'd never left the city, that if they'd stayed in Boston, everything would have been different. But I always felt guilty for saying it, because I knew he thought that different meant my mom might still be alive if we'd lived in a city where she didn't have to drive.

My dad was usually pretty good about stuff like my going to the mall for burgers. He wanted me to feel like a normal kid, especially after my mom died. Silas's parents were the heavy-duty vegetarians, the peace-and-love ex-hippies who hadn't let him have a TV when he was little and didn't let him play video games or eat lots of junk food—and look what had happened to him.

We'd all finished our burgers and fries. Avery was painting a picture with ketchup on the inside of a foil wrapper. And Silas was telling us—for the millionth time—about what happened when he and his mom and dad got called into Dr. Willner's office.

The reason was they'd found Silas's Mexican hash pipe during the random locker search.

Brian said, "Dude, if they searched *your* locker, maybe it wasn't so random."

I didn't want to think about that. Because if it wasn't random, why had they searched mine?

"You guys know that pipe," Silas said. "That

one that looks like a turtle? Carved out of some kind of pink stone?"

"All too well, my man," said Avery. "We know that pipe all too well."

"Well, the hard thing was convincing them I didn't know it was a pipe. I kept saying I thought it was some kind of Aztec ritual object. I said I bought it on the eighth grade class trip to the science museum in Boston. Nobody went for it, really. Dr. Willner sniffed the pipe and made a face and said he doubted it smelled that way when— and *if*—I bought it at the science museum.

"My dad said, 'Are you accusing my son of lying?'

"And Dr. Willner said, 'Not exactly,' in this icy Dracula voice that was so . . . so *threatening* that even my dad shut up. Which was totally demoralizing. I mean, I'd always assumed that when it came right down to it, my parents would stick up for me, no matter what."

I just listened. I couldn't stop thinking about

how, when Dr. Willner stepped out of his office and saw me with Silas, I'd tried to pretend that me and Silas weren't best friends, that we weren't as tight as we were.

"I don't know," Silas was saying. "I think Dr. Willner was working on getting my mom and dad so *anxious* about me, and about the depraved junkie psycho I was turning into, about my future, my 'drug problem,' my health . . . it was almost like they became the kids and Dr. Willner was the parent, and they needed him to help, to tell them what to do. My mom said, 'Silas, honey, are you sure you didn't get the pipe from another kid and maybe misremembered buying it in the science museum? Sometimes things like that happen . . .'

"'Sure,' I said. 'That could have happened . . . .'

"'I don't think it *did* happen,' Dr. Willner said. 'And I don't think you think so, either, Silas. But unfortunately, under the circumstances, there's nothing much we can do. Though we're hoping that the school policy will change in the near future, at the moment narcotics paraphernalia still does not come under the rubric of our Zero Tolerance guidelines.'"

By now Silas, like practically everybody in the school, could do such a dead-on imitation of our grief and crisis counselor that it was almost as if Silas had vacated his body and Dr. Willner had moved in. Plus he'd figured out how to do that special alarming expression that made you unsure if Dr. Willner was going to throw his arms around you or kick you in the head.

"'What I want you to understand, young man, is that we *will* be watching. And that if you *are* using drugs or any illegal substances at all, we will know, and we will find you, and you will be disciplined to the fullest extent of the law.'"

Each time Silas reached that part, the rest of us got very quiet. We felt the way he must have felt at the time, just before Willner set him loose—that is, basically relieved but extremely nervous. It seemed as if we'd all gone through his moment of hell in Willner's office. We couldn't help it; we looked around, up and over our shoulders, as if we were checking to see if Dr. Willner was spying on us through some secret peephole in the wall of Burger Heaven.

Eventually Brian said, "Silas, man, if I were you, I would totally clean up my act. Because they are going to find you, and they are going to get you, and, the way things are going, you are going to be dead meat."

I was glad that Brian cut to the chase. It was what we'd all been thinking. And also, to tell the truth, I think we'd all been feeling guilty about letting Silas turn into such a stoner without saying anything or stopping him. I guess we let it happen because it didn't directly hurt us. Actually it was worse than that: He was so entertaining and easy to make fun of when he got paranoid and a little crazy.

We should have said something a long time ago, long before Dr. Willner butted in. Because even if Silas *wasn't* busted—which, frankly, at this point was beginning to seem *fairly* unlikely—there was still the question of what he was doing to his brain. His gray matter would look like Swiss cheese when he was twenty or thirty if he'd been messing with his head like this since he was a kid.

"It's not so easy to just *quit*," Silas said. "Especially not now."

The rest of us looked at one another. That was *not* what we wanted to hear. We would much rather have gone on thinking that Silas could choose to get high or not, when and where he wanted. We would rather not have known that it was something he couldn't choose to stop.

I said, "Maybe you should join some group or—"

"Right," said Silas. "Give me a break. What would that group be? Sophomore Stoners Anonymous? Hi, my name is Silas, and I am a total pothead. Come on, guys, I don't think so. Look, I've got this thing handled. I can get it together on my own. It just might take a while."

"You haven't *got* a while," Avery said. "Willner's going to be all over you. Like jelly on peanut butter. Plus, what about Coach Pete? You missed the part where he announced that from now on random drug testing was actually going to mean *random*."

"Don't worry about Coach Pete," Silas said. "And don't worry about me. Trust me. Have I ever gone so far out that I couldn't get back?"

This didn't reassure us, exactly. We all just sat there and watched Avery make ketchup art on his burger wrapper. It looked like he was painting with blood. Until finally Brian said, "Hey, quit that, dude. It's disgusting."

That Sunday was the Harvest Fair at the Green Land Nursery, where Clara worked. Apple bobbing, cider pressing, hayrides for the little kids. It was totally ridiculous, a complete waste of time, but in the two years since my dad had been going out with Clara, he'd guilt tripped me into going with him both years.

I don't know why it meant so much to him. I guess because the whole town went to the Harvest Fair. People had nothing else to do on that particular weekend. Or *ever*, for that matter, considering where we lived and how little was going on there. Everyone in the area went, everyone but my friends. In general it was not the kind of event at which high-school kids were dying to hang out, trailing along behind their parents and standing there, grinning like retards when their parents ran into people they knew, people they had nothing to say to, except how much the kids had grown since last year's Harvest Fair.

I guess that was part of the reason my dad wanted me to go. All the people he knew went, and they all knew he was going out with Clara. He felt it would have *meant* something if I blew the whole thing off, that it would be my way of telling the entire world that I didn't like him being with Clara.

Of course, this was all in my dad's mind. It was strange, how when it came to certain subjects, my dad could think like an insecure teenager. So, in this case, he assumed that people were watching, judging, focused on how much I liked or didn't like Clara, when in fact no one was paying the slightest attention at all. The truth was that no one would have noticed if I went to the Harvest Fair or not. They were too busy fighting with their own kids, or seeing who'd gotten a new car that year, maybe a better car than they had, or wiping the sticky trails of jelly-apple goo off the kinder-garteners' faces. But I had to go and be miserable, wandering around with nothing to do except think how much my mom would have hated Harvest Fair.

She'd never had to go to it. It started the year after she died, and it was where my dad met Clara.

My mom liked to garden, but she always ordered seeds and bulbs from catalogs. One of the things that was great about her was that she hated shopping. And that's really what people were doing at the Harvest Fair, shopping for pots of chrysanthemums and packages of pumpkin leaf bags and those stupid wreaths made from dead leaves and cornstalks. Obviously that's why Green Land had the fair in the first place. Green Land hadn't gotten to be the most successful nursery in western Massachusetts by holding free nonprofit "community events" just to be neighborly. That was what my mom would have said. She hated "events" like that.

"Come on, all your friends will be there," Dad said.

"*None* of my friends will be there," I said. "Their *parents* will be there. *Their* parents aren't making *them* go." Didn't he realize that I was too old to be conned into doing things like this? I knew better than to say that. Because if I did, then my dad would get really depressing and say, I know. I know. You're growing up. I'll only have you with me for a few more years. After that you'll be free to do whatever you want. So just do this for me now.

"Come on," said Dad. "You never know. You might have fun."

I said, "Dad, I will *not* have fun. I'm not going. Last year was enough. That's it."

Dad said, "Tom, how often do I ask you to do anything for *me*?"

I had to admit: not often. Still, it annoyed me that he said that whenever he wanted me to do *anything*.

My dad said, "Come on. It's a beautiful day. What else were you planning to do? Stay inside and watch TV? Surf the Internet?"

"I have homework," I said. And then I tried to remember if I actually did. A one-page paper for Mrs. Ridley on the War of 1812. And some crummy story in the reader to skim for English class.

"You could have done your homework yesterday," Dad said. "When you had the time to spend all day at the mall."

"No one does homework on Saturday," I said.

But it was over. He'd won.

• • •

On the way to Harvest Fair, I tried to convince
myself that maybe it wouldn't be so bad. But as we
pulled into the driveway, and I saw the crowd, the
irritating grade-school kids, the dressed-up yup-
pie parents, weekenders from the city, plus all the
people I'd known forever, the guy from the post
office, the woman from the supermarket, all
strolling over the green lawns, chatting, running
around, stopping to kiss and say hi, I knew that it
would be worse than whatever I'd imagined.

As luck would have it, Brian's parents were getting out of their Land Rover just as Dad and I were
getting out of our Celica. Somehow having them
see me made my being there seem even more
embarrassing. It was degrading that my dad had
talked me into it, whereas Brian's parents, as I
knew, had briefly tried and failed. I took some
comfort in the fact that I knew something they
didn't: Brian was spending the afternoon with
Andrea, and they were probably having sex. Brian's

dad was a film director, his mother was an artist. Their house was even fancier than their car. Brian's dad was kind of a jerk, but I liked his mom. I like how she still wore sunglasses and black leather.

She was the only mom who kissed me, a confident but absentminded peck on the cheek that I certainly preferred to the warm sloppy hug and the heavy eye contact I could count on from Silas's mom. First Brian's mom kissed me, then my dad.

"How's school?" she asked.

"Weird," I said.

"So I hear." Brian's mom turned to my dad. "That's what Brian's been saying."

"That's more information than I get out of Tom," said Dad. "When I ask Tom how school is, he always says, 'Fine.'"

I shot my dad a dirty look. He knew that wasn't true. I had been trying to tell him how weird school was, but he always put me off with that crap about how the school was doing its best, trying to keep us safe. I thought about Silas's parents rolling over for Dr. Willner. What my dad had just done was one of my least favorite habits of his: the way he'd sell me out just to get a laugh from his friends. My mom had never done that, and a couple of times she even got down on my dad for making some lame little joke at my expense.

"Brian got random drug tested," she said. "So it looks like I'm paying thousands of dollars a year in school taxes so my son can urinate in a paper cup while some pervert watches. Isn't that outrageous?"

Coach Pete wasn't a pervert! Did I have to point that out? I kept quiet and told myself that the pervert she meant was Dr. Willner.

"Outrageous," agreed Brian's dad, but with the air of someone who hadn't been listening and hears just one word and is trying to catch up with the drift of the conversation.

"And those *vile* e-mails. One insane new rule after another. As if none of us had anything to do but read that poison they spew into cyberspace. The parents have got to do *something*. We need to talk," Brian's mom told my dad. "I'll call you."

"Do that," my dad said. "Let me know."

"Catch you later." Brian's dad mouthed the words back over his shoulder.

I was glad that at least some of the parents were paying attention to what was going on at school.

I said, "See, Dad? I told you. I can't believe you told Brian's mom that I've been saying school was fine."

But my dad had already moved on and was trying to find Clara. Finally he saw her talking to an elderly couple, selling them a shrub so hard you would have thought it was a Mercedes. The autumn sun shining through her curly blond hair reminded me of something I couldn't quite place. Then I remembered: Becca's hair. Clara's cheeks were pink, as usual. Even in the summer she looked as if she'd just come in from the cold.

I lagged behind as my dad sped up, as if he were being pulled toward her by some gravitational force. Then I stopped and watched. Clara looked up and saw my dad—and her face lit up. Basically I was glad that my dad was with her. But it made me feel shut out, as if we'd been playing musical chairs, and they'd grabbed the last two seats. The two of them kissed lightly.

"Hi, Clara," I said.

"Hi, Tom, what's up?"

"The nursery looks really cool," I said. I wasn't exactly lying, but I obviously didn't believe that a few scarecrows and pumpkins and cornstalks had transformed Green Land into some scenic autumn garden spot. Still, I knew that she'd been working late every night for the past week, getting the place ready. I wanted to say something nice. And that was it, the end of the line, we'd run out of things to say.

"Okay, see you at dinner," I said.

My dad and Clara exchanged uneasy looks. Then my dad said, "I told you that you were invited to the party at Arthur's, didn't I?" Clara's boss, Arthur, was a lawyer who owned Green Land on the side. "We'd love to have you come along."

"That's okay," I said. "I don't think so." My dad didn't even try. For one thing, that *we* was a big mistake. For another, the fact that I'd agreed to come to Harvest Fair didn't leave him much slack for conning me into going to Arthur's party. I said, "I'll see you guys in a little while."

"Here's ten bucks," said my dad. "Don't spend it all in one place."

Normally ten bucks would have seemed pretty cheesy for a whole afternoon, but it was fine for Harvest Fair. There was nothing to buy, anyway. I wandered around for as long as I could stand it. There was nothing to look at. Every so often, someone my dad knew would stop me to tell me how much I'd grown since last year. It was worse than no one talking to me at all.

Finally I bought a cup of hot cider and a cinnamon doughnut. I found a bench on the edge of the forest and sat down facing the woods. I put the doughnut on the bench and drank the cider first.

The cider was great. The perfect temperature, the perfect amount of sweetness. I liked how the cup felt between my hands, I liked drinking the warm liquid. Even so, I didn't feel right. Maybe it was the forest, how beautiful it was, the bright coins of sunlight shining on the yellow and orange leaves. I thought of everything that was wrong, starting with my mom being dead, then school being so messed up. . . . I felt like I was tumbling down into a pit, and I had to get my balance and stop falling. I picked up the doughnut and I decided to eat it in the tiniest pieces, crumb by crumb, and not waste one grain of sugar or one speck of cinnamon.

That took up a very long time. I only had a few crumbs left when my dad finally found me.

"I was worried about you," he said.

"Worried about *what*?" I said. "I was here all the time. What did you think happened?" It made me angry when my dad still acted as if I were some toddler who could just wander off or get kidnapped or somehow disappear. Meanwhile, a kid I knew *had* disappeared. Stephanie Tyrone. And if Silas didn't clean up his act, he might be next. Why couldn't my dad get it right and figure out what to be nervous about? Why wasn't he worried about *that*?

"I don't know what I thought," he said. "I just got anxious when I couldn't find you. Sorry. Okay. I'll drive you home. I'll meet Clara at Arthur's later. That is, if it's okay with you for me to go to Arthur's."

"Why wouldn't it be okay with me? Have a ball," I told him. "I've got homework. Like I said."

Halfway to the parking lot, Clara caught up with us. "I'll walk you out to the car," she said. "Arthur's sprung me for five minutes from the shrub detail."

My dad walked between the two of us, with his arms around our shoulders. It would have hurt his feelings to pull away, and besides, I didn't want to. People smiled at us as they passed, and actually it felt good for a little while to have strangers think we were a family. Which we weren't.

It was all very confusing, so I stopped looking at people's faces and concentrated on the gravel skittering out from under our feet. Which was why I didn't see Dr. Willner until we almost had a head-on collision.

As soon as I saw him, I stopped short, and my dad and Clara stopped, too. It was disturbing, seeing Dr. Willner out in the world, and it was even more bizarre to see him wearing a black-and-red-checked hunting jacket. I thought of *The Catcher in the Rye*—those were the colors of Holden's hat—and of Dr. Willner telling me to take the book home and destroy it. It struck me that it was the same thing that Mrs. Ridley told Becca about her paper. I suddenly couldn't remember where I'd left the book. In my backpack, I thought. Maybe. Had Dr. Willner forgotten that red was the forbidden color? Or didn't that rule apply to him?

But the weirdest thing of all was that Dr. Willner was with his wife. I mean, it was weird that he *had* a wife. Though actually she was exactly what you'd imagine—mousy, plain, terrified looking—if someone told you Willner was married. Plus she looked about twenty years older than Dr. Willner.

Dr. Willner's gaze bounced off me as if he'd never seen me before. I had the creepy feeling that Dr. Willner didn't appreciate my running into him, outside of school, out in the world, in his hunting jacket, and especially with his wife. And I thought that this was another thing he would make me pay for. Then he moved on to my dad, and I got the chills remembering how he'd said he was eager to meet my father. At last his gaze froze on Clara, and his mouth twitched slightly—a tiny tic that was as close to a smile as I'd seen him manage.

"Nice to see you," he told Clara.

"Nice to see *you*," she told him and his wife. My dad and I nodded and smiled, and we passed them and kept walking.

"How do you know Dr. Willner?" I asked Clara.

She said, "Is that his name? What a horrible freak. That poor wife stopped by last week and bought a potted amaryllis. Maybe it cost ten, eleven bucks, not exactly a major purchase. It would have been lovely when it bloomed, big pink blossoms in the dead of winter. And the next day he came in with her, and he *made* her return it, and the most humiliating thing was he made her insist that we give her back *cash*. The poor thing had tears in her eyes. It was totally disgusting."

"Who *is* that guy?" said Dad.

"He's the one I've been telling you about," I said. "Our grief and crisis counselor."

"What grief?" said Clara. "What crisis?"

"I told you guys," I said, though suddenly, I couldn't remember how much I'd actually told them and how much I'd just *thought* about telling them. "He's sort of taken over—ever since Pleasant Valley." And then, though I knew it wasn't the right moment and that the middle of the parking lot was hardly the right place, I said, "He's the guy who busted me for reading *The Catcher in the Rye* in school."

"I don't understand," said my dad. "Wasn't it an assignment?"

"No," I said. "I guess it's not in the curriculum anymore. I was reading it on my own. And Dr. Willner told me I wasn't even allowed to have a copy in my locker."

I held my breath. It was almost as if I'd just lit a firecracker and was waiting for it to explode. I waited—but nothing happened.

My dad sighed deeply and said, "So fine. Read it at home." He sounded, I don't know. Tired. And it struck me that maybe he had a lot of things on his mind: me. Clara. Some editor giving him a hard time about the way he was drawing beans. And probably, still, my mom. I sympathized, I understood how he could have felt worn out. But I didn't have to like it. I needed him to pull it together. He could be tired—but not asleep. I needed him to wake up.

six

MONDAY I STAYED HOME with a pretend sore throat. My dad knew I was faking. But he was nice about it. He understood that I hardly ever pulled stuff like that.

I just wasn't ready to go back to school yet. I needed a little break. And besides, I hadn't written my War of 1812 one-pager for Mrs. Ridley. On Sunday night, when my dad went to meet Clara at Arthur's, I'd goofed off, watched TV, and played video games.

No one talked much on the bus anymore. Tuesday, when I got on, my friends were slumped in their seats, watching Bus TV. It was a "Great Moments" about the Civil War. It said that the founding fathers from up north voted unanimously to prohibit slavery in the Constitution, and that the southerners voted them down. Why were we all watching this? I guess because it was on.

Maybe if we'd talked instead of watched TV, my friends would have warned me, told me what the new rules were—and saved me a lot of trouble.

When I got to school that morning, the guard we all called Bug Boy gave my backpack a thorough and energetic examination. He grabbed my cell phone and said, "Aha! No cell phones for any reason!"

"But I have a note from my dad," I said. "He needs to be able to reach me."

"No cell phones for *any* reason," Bug Boy repeated. And he threw my phone in the bin. I thought how expensive and how much trouble this was going to be, and how steamed my dad would be when he found out. This might be the final straw that brought him into school to complain. I decided not to tell my dad until he asked or tried to call me. After my big bombshell about *The Catcher in the Rye* had fizzled out, I decided to wait awhile before I put my dad through any more tests.

In the front office all the secretaries were busy. It took forever for anyone to notice me standing there, waiting to get the pass I needed in order to be readmitted to class.

Assembly had already begun by the time I arrived. I got there just in time to hear Dr. Willner congratulating the students on how they had complied with the no-cell-phones-for-any-reason rule, which he had announced yesterday and which had gone into effect this morning.

I'd talked to Avery on the phone last night. Why hadn't he mentioned it? And what about my dad? Had he lost interest and stopped reading the e-mails from school?

"That is," said Dr. Willner, "*most* of you have complied. There were, as always, a few holdouts, a couple of brilliant students who were a little . . . slow to get with the program, or who thought that they could get *away* with something, or who imagined that they knew better than the authorities. Our guards were instructed to seize all phones, and these seizures have gone into these students' permanent records."

Once more I had the feeling that he had singled me out of the auditorium and was looking directly at me. I wondered if he had the knack of making all the kids feel that way. I also wondered if I should bother making sure someone knew that I was out sick yesterday and hadn't heard about the new rule, and so I couldn't be blamed for Bug Boy finding the phone in my pack this morning. But probably I would have had to explain this directly to Dr. Willner, and the idea exhausted me. The truth was, it hardly seemed worth it.

"And that's it," concluded Dr. Willner. "After this—after this *moment*—there will be Zero Tolerance for cell-phone use in school. Of any kind. Simple possession will, as always, result in an automatic two-day suspension."

It was a miracle there was anybody at *all* left in school, what with the long lists that changed every day, the gigantic catalog of all the things that could get you thrown out. Or maybe the miracle was that every time a new rule came into effect, kids started following it right away. If this went on long enough, it was going to turn even the wimpiest nerds into the kind of psycho killers who shot up the gym at Pleasant Valley.

The funny thing was, school did seem a little emptier—a little less crowded—than it used to be, though we couldn't think of anybody who'd left, anyone who used to be here and wasn't anymore. Anybody, that is, except Stephanie Tyrone. No one had heard from Stephanie since her family supposedly moved to another part of the country. Her friends had tried to call and e-mail her, but she didn't answer. People were saying it was as if she'd vanished off the face of the earth.

After assembly we trudged off to social studies class. I handed in my paper, and Mrs. Ridley began the lesson. It had been so long since we'd started off with a class discussion of what we'd seen in the news that we'd almost forgotten that it used to happen. What was that question she used to ask? "Is there anyone who would like to bring up a topic of general interest?" I was pretty sure that was it. But I could hardly remember.

No one was listening very hard as Mrs. Ridley told us how Dolley Madison had saved something or other from the burning White House.

She said, "Imagine, students, the bravery that was required for her to put the good of the nation before her own *individual* well-being."

Why did Mrs. Ridley look so strange when she said that word individual? I dimly remembered how, at the start of the year, she'd said that one reason we were studying American history and the Constitution was so we would understand how much our ancestors had gone through to guarantee our individual freedoms. And now she was making individual sound like something suspect, and antisocial. But maybe I was remembering wrong, maybe I was confused. It seemed like too much trouble to try and figure it out. I stopped listening and looked out the window at the trees, which hardly had any leaves.

Almost no one was listening to her. And so because we were all so spaced out, gazing out the window, dreaming about this or that, it took us a long time to register what we were hearing:

A cell phone was ringing inside someone's backpack.

It rang for what seemed like hours. Nobody moved a muscle. Didn't the person have an answering function? And whose cell phone was it?

You couldn't tell from anyone's face. *Everybody* looked guilty and scared. Maybe everybody was wondering if they'd forgotten and brought theirs in by mistake.

I was thinking—and I'm sure other kids were, too—of that day, a million years ago, when everybody's cell phones rang at once. And it had been our parents calling, with the bad news about Pleasant Valley.

The phone wouldn't stop ringing. Who was calling? And who was being called? How had the person managed to get through the backpack search this morning? But in fact, it wasn't difficult. They didn't always search everyone. In this case, random *meant* random.

The phone rang and rang, until finally Mrs. Ridley said, "Will someone answer that, please?" She looked as horrified as the rest of us. She couldn't believe that this had to happen in *her* class.

Only then did Becca Sawyer reach into her backpack.

"Hello?" she said. "Hello? Hello?"

We all stopped and watched and waited.

"It's nobody," she said at last. "Nobody's there."

Brian said, just loud enough for the class to hear, "It's probably Dr. Willner."

That shocked Mrs. Ridley out of the semitrance she'd slipped into when the phone started ringing. Probably the rule was that she was supposed to send Becca straight to Dr. Willner's office, with the illegal phone and the note that would get her suspended. But it was obvious from her expression that she couldn't bring herself to do it.

After all, it was *Becca*. All the teachers loved her. Becca had never had a mark on *her* spotless permanent record. And yet I had the feeling that Mrs. Ridley would have been going through the same hell no matter whose phone it was. You could watch the struggle going on in her face, as if an angel and a devil were tugging in opposite directions.

Eventually the angel won.

"Class," she said. "Here's what we're going to do. This never happened. Becca's phone never rang. None of you ever heard it. This whole incident did not occur. No one will mention it, ever. And no one will ever, *ever* bring a phone into school again. Class, do I have your word on this?"

"Yes," said everyone at once.

"Hold up your hands if you promise," Mrs. Ridley said. And we all raised our hands. Suddenly

I noticed how hard my heart was beating, and it felt like everyone's heart was beating in unison. Everybody's heart—including Mrs. Ridley's—was pounding and speeding and doing that same trippy thing at once.

Somehow we got through the rest of class. When the bell rang, we all looked at one another, as if we were searching our classmates' eyes to see what the proper expression might be. Then we were afraid to look anymore, and we went out into the school.

By the end of the day we'd almost made ourselves forget about it, as though nothing ever happened. But every time I spotted Becca, she looked paler than she had before. I tried to give her an encouraging smile, but somehow my face wouldn't work. I almost wanted to put my arm around her, but there were always other kids watching.

The next morning, when we got to social studies class, Mrs. Ridley wasn't there. She'd never been late before. We waited until ten minutes after the bell. We sat up very straight in our chairs. We were absolutely silent. Every so often Brian, Avery, Silas, and I would look at one another and roll our eyes in a way that meant: Uh-oh. This isn't good.

Finally Mrs. Davis, our algebra teacher, came into the room. She said that Mrs. Ridley had been taken ill with a sudden health emergency, and that she would be taking over the class until a permanent replacement or substitute teacher was found.

It took a couple of minutes for us to understand what she'd said, and then a few minutes more for the full implications of this to sink in. Once more we sat there like statues. No one had the courage to look at anyone else. We certainly couldn't look at Becca. Not that we thought that it was her fault, exactly. But we knew that she probably thought so.

None of us believed for one second the "health emergency" story. I mean, it all seemed a little too neat, a little too convenient. One day Mrs. Ridley suggests we don't tell anyone about Becca breaking a new school rule—and the next day she gets so sick she doesn't come to class?

No one listened to a word Mrs. Davis said. We had too much else on our minds. Because, one by one, we were starting to figure out that this could only mean one thing. Someone—one of *us*—had told Dr. Willner about Becca's phone, and about Mrs. Ridley instructing us to keep it secret. The spy had to be a student who, as Dr. Willner said, was "ahead of the curve." Or else they had bugs and hidden cameras everywhere, and someone had been watching.

It turned out that my dad was still reading at least some of his e-mails from school, because that same night, he got one suggesting that parents encourage students to report any suspicious or illegal behavior on the part of their classmates. Anyone who made a threat, even in jest, anyone who talked about violence, anyone who used drugs or had a gun, anything out of the ordinary—should be reported promptly.

The message said that such precautions might have averted the tragedy at Pleasant Valley. Apparently lots of kids there knew in advance that the kids who did the shootings were planning something terrible, but they just thought the killers were boasting or trying to make themselves seem cool.

That seemed peculiar, because the story we'd heard first—the version that had been on the news—was that none of the Pleasant Valley kids had ever paid any attention to the killers or even knew their names or who they were. I was thinking like Avery now, super reasonable and legally minded. I tried to remember to tell Avery this when I saw him on the bus the next morning.

My dad printed out the message, brought it into the living room, and gave it to me to read.

"So?" I said. "What am I supposed to do about

this? Turn in anyone who makes a joke about Pleasant Valley?"

I had the feeling that I knew about a million suspicious things that I was now supposed to report. But fortunately I couldn't remember what any of them were—not that I would have reported anyone anyway. For a moment I was confused. Was my dad telling me to get with the program? That would have been so unlike him. That would have really alarmed me.

"Nothing." My dad sounded angry. "You're not supposed to do anything at all. I just thought you ought to know what kind of toxic crap they're putting out. You should know that you probably need to watch out and be careful what you say. Once they start encouraging kids to tell on other kids, anything can happen, anybody can say anything. But the point is, Tomster, no matter what you see, no matter what you hear, or what you know, no matter how you're pressured, I don't want you to knuckle under, or to be anything less than a totally stand-up guy. I didn't raise my kid to be the kind of person who'd rat on his friends. No matter what."

It made me incredibly happy. Maybe he wasn't about to go in and slug it out with Dr. Willner, but he was still my dad. He hadn't zoned out completely. And only now that it no longer seemed like a possibility, only now could I admit to myself what had really scared me: that my dad could change, like the teachers had, that somehow he could be turned into a pod person—like they'd tried, and almost succeeded, in doing to poor Mrs. Ridley.

"Don't worry. I wouldn't tell on anyone even if I knew anything," I said. "And besides, I *don't* know anything. Maybe my friends don't have the world's best attitude, but they're not doing anything wrong."

I thought, Well, okay, not *much* wrong. Silas was still getting loaded. And probably we could all have gotten turned in for saying half the stuff we said, on a daily basis, about the guards and Dr. Willner. Which is probably why I sounded like I was lying. Anyway, it hardly made any difference what we were or weren't doing. I knew it was only a matter of time until one or all of us got into really big trouble.

seven

MAYBE IF MRS. RIDLEY hadn't gotten fired or had a "health emergency" and vanished forever, things might have turned out differently. Maybe Coach Pete wouldn't have felt pressured into random-testing Silas. He probably knew, like we did, how the test was going to turn out. Still, with his own wife working for Dr. Willner, and with Mrs. Ridley's disappearance making it very clear what happened to teachers who disobeyed the new rules and regulations, Coach Pete didn't have much choice. There wasn't much else he could do, and we didn't blame him. It was like a tragedy. What happened had to happen.

Coach Pete tried, he honestly did. He saved Silas till last to be tested. He gave him the most time, the maximum possible warning. And maybe the school knew about *that*, too, and was giving him a hard time, reminding him that once again he was defeating the whole purpose of random testing.

Finally one afternoon, just before practice began, Coach Pete sighed a deep sigh and said, "Okay, Silas, my man, let's do it."

Silas said, "Oh, man, couldn't we wait *one* day? I mean . . . maybe two or three days?"

Which essentially *was* the test, right there. Silas had already failed. After that, it was just a matter of making it official.

The coach and Silas were gone a long time. A very, *very* long time. Maybe Silas couldn't make himself piss in the cup. Maybe the coach was repeating the test in the hopes that the stick might come out a different color. Or maybe he was trying to think of some way out, of something else he could do. But by then there was no way out.

The two of them reappeared, but just for a minute. It was obvious what had happened.

Coach Pete said, "Let's bag practice for this afternoon. See you guys tomorrow, same time, same place. Silas and I have some business I guess we need to take care of."

He couldn't look us in the eye. Not that he had to, really. Because we were all watching Silas, whose face was as white as paper.

After Silas and the coach left, we just stood there with our mouths open, the Smart and Dumb Jocks alike.

Finally Brian said, "Silas knew this was coming. What the hell was he *thinking*?"

Avery said, "We warned the dude a million times. He *knew* it would go down this way."

We all knew that Silas had really been dumb. Unless he *wanted* to get caught. There was always that possibility. But still, it didn't seem right to blame him. First because he was our friend. And second because we had no idea what was going to happen to him now.

• • •

It wasn't as if they started those places after the shootings at Pleasant Valley. They'd had them for a long time, we'd all seen them on TV, these torture camps where they put kids with drug and behavior problems. Okay, not torture camps. Nature programs. "Survival school." Fifteen days in the desert with a thermos of water and some crazed, goofy ex-marine barking commando orders at you. The reason we'd all heard of them was that every so often some kid died in a place like that, and *60 Minutes* did an installment.

We knew those places existed. But it was different when your friend was going to some nightmare hell in Arizona.

Operation Turnaround.

That was what Dr. Willner and Silas's parents decided: that it was in Silas's best interests, that a month at Operation Turnaround was the only way he would ever wake up and see the light. The only way he could change his bad habits was to go out to the wilderness and nearly die of thirst and exhaustion and exposure while some maniac forced him to hike through the desert in the hottest part of the day. No phone calls, no e-mail, no letters, no TV, no contact with the outside world except for a weekly telephone call to his parents, and even that would be monitored by the Operation Turnaround staff.

We didn't think Silas needed to change. He was basically a good guy. He just needed to stop smoking so much weed. Silas's dad had a bit of a drinking problem, if you want to know the truth, but no one ever sent him to boot camp in the desert.

I couldn't believe that Silas's mom had gone for it, no matter how much Dr. Willner tried to make his parents believe that his future—his mental health—depended on his being sent away. His mom had been friends with *my* mom. She wasn't the kind of person to let her own kid get shipped off to some prison colony in the middle of the desert. It was as if she'd become someone else. Who knew what Dr. Willner had threatened them with? Jail time, maybe. Something worse. But what could have been worse than jail time?

Silas wouldn't tell us what happened in Dr. Willner's office. But then he wasn't saying much at all—he *couldn't* say much—when we went to visit him at home. That was the only way we were allowed to see him. He was under house arrest until his mom and dad put him on the plane for Arizona.

Brian, Avery, and I went to Silas's on that last Saturday afternoon before he left for the desert. We could only spend half an hour, and Silas's mom had to be present. No unsupervised visits were permitted. Dr. Willner had made that clear.

Silas's mom gave us big, sloppy hugs. We braced ourselves for the big stare, that relentless icky eye contact she always insisted on making. But now she didn't look at us at all as she air kissed the empty space around our faces. She kept offering us snacks, things to eat and drink. Sodas, pretzels—all the junk food she never let Silas have before he was being punished. So maybe she *had* become someone else. It certainly seemed that way. None of us were hungry, but we kept saying yes, so that she'd keep leaving the living room so we could talk to Silas.

But Silas wasn't talking. He shook his head, then opened his mouth, then shook his head again. He was like some stroke or accident victim who could still see and think and hear but who'd lost the power of speech.

"Man," he kept saying. "Man. This is bad."

Brian asked him what had happened in Dr. Willner's office. Silas shook his head.

"Dude, what happened? Did they, like, *torture* you?"

"Not physically," said Silas.

There was a silence that lasted so long that, for a moment, I was scared it would never end. We all looked to Silas to say something, which made no sense, since he was in the worst shape of anyone. But finally Silas did talk. He said, "Want to watch a tape?"

I didn't, and it was clear that no one else

wanted to, either. I couldn't imagine concentrating or even sitting still long enough to watch a tape, to say nothing of the fact that we could only stay half an hour, and it felt weird to spend the minutes we had left zoned out in front of the tube. Still, it seemed to be something Silas wanted, and at least it would be better than sitting there saying nothing. So we said sure, man, yeah, that would be great, what tape do you have in mind?

Silas slid a tape in, and the opening credits came up. It was *Invasion of the Body Snatchers.*

"Oh, man, we've seen this a million times," said Brian.

"Then one more won't kill us," I said. I didn't want to watch it, either, but I knew that Silas wanted us to.

"Brian's right," said Silas's mom. "You boys have seen this so often. I can never understand how you can watch the same film over and over."

No one answered her. It would have seemed as if we were taking her side against Silas.

After we'd been watching for only a few seconds—the Kevin McCarthy character had just jumped out in front of the car—Silas's mom said, "I don't think this is a good idea. Films like this are so bad for you, honey. It's just this kind of paranoid thinking that got you into trouble in the first place. Just a few nights ago, we got an e-mail from school telling us to be extra careful about what films and tapes you kids watched. Now I'm going to get you boys some more snacks and when I come back in, let's turn this tape off, okay? It's such a pity to spend your last time together just passively watching a movie."

Silas's mom left and came back in with a bowl of potato chips and a bottle of ginger ale and some glasses on a tray. She passed the bowl around, and each of us, including Silas, took one chip apiece, just to be polite.

"Have more, please, boys." Silas's mom turned off the VCR.

"No, thanks, that's okay," said Brian.

"When do you leave, man?" said Avery.

"Tomorrow morning," Silas said. But we knew that already.

"Look at the bright side," Avery said. "No more boring math class. No more Dr. Willner. Plus, winter's coming, and it's warm out there—"

Avery shouldn't have said that. Silas started to cry. Not sobbing or wailing or anything. Just fat tears welling up out of his eyes and rolling down his cheeks.

We had no idea what do to. It was like a funeral, it was like someone had died. Except that the dead person was sitting there crying and crumbling his potato chip. I was so afraid I was going to cry, too, that I took a sip of soda and closed my eyes.

When I opened them again, Silas was still crying. We looked at Silas's mom, as if we were hoping she would make us feel better or at least tell us what to do. But, weirdly, she was smiling.

"What's everyone so gloomy about?" Silas's mom asked. "This is only for a month. Then Silas is coming back, and everything will be fine. And Dr. Willner promised that if Silas stays drug-free until the end of the school year, none of this will go down on his permanent record."

"That sounds great," Avery lied. In fact, a month sounded like a very long time, especially if you were going to spend it crawling through the desert and learning to survive on beef jerky and cactus juice.

Then suddenly Silas said, very loud, "I'm never coming back! That's what you people don't understand. They'll ship me off to that place. And you'll never hear from me again."

"Silas, dear," said his mother. "We understand you're uneasy about this. We're all a little nervous. But soon we'll all be together back home again."

"They're lying to you," said Silas. "You don't understand. And what you *really* don't understand is that this isn't happening just here at Central. Stuff like this is happening at schools all over the country. Kids are disappearing, and they're never heard from again!"

"How do you know this?" said Avery.

"E-mail," said Silas. "Chat rooms. Kid from different parts of the country are talking about it. There are all these new web sites: www. freedom-forteens.com. And: www.teensfightback.com. Check it out, dudes. And it's really dangerous for the people who post this stuff, because—"

"They're talking about *what* things?" said Avery. "Metal detectors? Drug tests? They've had that at other schools for years! Central High was lucky for a really long time. It had to happen, sooner or later. And those rehab camps have been *around*, man—"

Silas ignored him. "—dangerous because they're reading these people's e-mails, and sending them away. These web sites and chat rooms are all talking about concentration camps for kids. Like Operation Turnaround. Kids check in, and they don't check out."

Everyone fell so silent there was nothing to do but listen to the ticking of the gold clock on Silas's mantelpiece.

"A wedding present," said Silas's mom nonsensically. Was she losing it or what? Then she said, "Silas, darling, that is just the sort of paranoid thinking that will get so much better once the drugs are out of your system. If you would just read the nightly e-mails from school instead of these disturbing . . . stories kids are making up. I mean, you know how kids are. . . ."

For some reason, that seemed like a signal to get up and leave.

We all hugged Silas, one by one. Silas had stopped crying, maybe for our benefit, so we wouldn't start crying, too.

"It's like Stalin," Silas said. "Check it out, dude. I'm not kidding. Do me a favor. Read up on Stalin and how he took control. Promise me you will."

Avery said, "Dude, we *know* who Stalin was, okay?"

"Promise me," said Silas.

I promised. Brian and Avery sort of grunted. That was all there was to say. We knew it was time to go.

"Take it easy, man," we said. "Take care, dude." "See you soon."

And then a weird thing happened. Silas's mom left the room, possibly so we'd have a few seconds together, or possibly just to position herself to say good-bye to us at the front door. As soon as she was gone, Silas got kind of wild-eyed. He grabbed the tape box that *Invasion of the Body Snatchers* had come in. He pointed to it, and he pointed in the general direction of his mom. He pointed to it again, and he pointed to his mom.

I said, "Man, what are you *saying* here? Are you kidding?" But I didn't think he was.

Before Silas could answer, his mom's voice drifted in from the hall.

"Boys," she called sweetly. "Come along. It's really time to get going."

eight

IGHT AFTER THAT the weather changed. It was as if Silas's absence made everything go cold and gray, as if his not being there caused the first snow to start falling. We'd known we were going to miss him, but it was shocking how much we did.

For a while we talked about Silas almost constantly, as if our just saying his name somehow meant he was still with us. We discussed how unfair it was, his being sent away. And we tried to imagine what he would have said about this or that. Then we stopped talking about him. Then we started again. We kept saying that it would be only a while, that he'd be back right after Thanksgiving—or anyway, before Christmas. But even that was horrifying, as we imagined ourselves enjoying turkey dinner in our warm houses with our families while

Silas, or so we imagined, was surviving on bread and water and sleeping in a tent in the desert, listening to the coyotes howling in the night.

We'd always known that Silas was a funny guy, but we hadn't realized how funny. Without him, all our jokes fell flat. Nothing made us laugh. It leached the fun out of everything. Everyone dug in and slouched down in their seats and watched Bus TV and waited for Dr. Willner to tell us what we couldn't do next.

It was spooky, what Silas had said about kids being sent away all over the country. That very same day we'd visited him, we went back to Brian's house and surfed the net, looking for the web sites and chat rooms Silas had told us about. But even Avery—who could usually track down *anything* on the net—couldn't find a word about it. Every time we tried logging on to the sites, we'd get messages that said SITE NO LONGER EXISTS. SITE REDIRECTED. But it was impossible to figure out where any of them had been redirected *to*.

And still we didn't believe it. It was just too weird to be true. Why wasn't it on the news? Why weren't parents complaining that their kids had disappeared? Probably another reason we couldn't believe it was true was that we didn't want to; we hoped it *wasn't* true. We didn't need any conspiracy theories to make us more nervous. What had happened was bad enough: Silas had tested positive for weed and been sent to a rehab center in Arizona.

When I told my dad, he said, "Let me get this straight. Silas has been sent off to one of those punishment camps in the desert—for smoking *marijuana?*" I'd always had a feeling that my dad used to get high when he was young. But he never said so, I didn't want to know, and this certainly didn't seem like the smartest moment to ask.

"Isn't that the dreadful place we saw on *Sixty Minutes?*" Clara said.

I'd decided to tell Dad and Clara at the same time, one night when Clara was over for dinner. I wanted to get both their reactions at once. And both of them were outraged, which was reassuring. Basically, I'd known that was how they'd react, but it was getting harder to be sure about anything. I never would have imagined that Silas's mom would go along with the program, either. The images I couldn't get out of my mind were of the weird smile she'd had when she talked about Silas going away, and of Silas pointing to the *Body Snatchers* tape and then pointing to his mom. What if my dad started smiling like that?

"I don't think it's the same one," said my dad. "But I don't know. What's that place called again?"

"Operation Turnaround," I said.

"Ugh. Just the name gives me the creeps," Clara said. "Operation Brainwash."

My dad said, "What's wrong with Silas's parents? Have they lost their *minds*? Imagine them agreeing to let their kid go off to one of those hellholes! That poor kid! No wonder he's got a drug problem! If *my* parents were like that—"

"I think they were scared," I said. "I think Dr. Willner persuaded them that Silas was in real trouble, that he was definitely going to wind up in jail or the mental hospital or somewhere—and that they should try this first."

I couldn't believe what was coming out of my mouth. Why was I defending Silas's parents? Maybe because I felt as if my dad was doing this thing he sometimes did, this habit which always annoyed me—putting down other kids' parents so as to make himself look good, to make me realize what a terrific dad *he* was, at least compared to the others. This was not the greatest time for him to get competitive with Silas's mother and father.

I couldn't bring myself to repeat what Silas had said—about the nationwide conspiracy against kids, about kids vanishing and not coming back, about his mom having been taken over by the pod people. The last thing I wanted was to make Silas sound totally crazy, as if they'd had a good reason for sending him away. Also, I think some supersititious part of me was worried that if I even mentioned the chance that Silas was really in danger, my saying it would somehow make it come true.

Clara said, "Still. Can you imagine your dad and me *ever* letting you be sent to someplace like that?"

What was this "your dad and me"? What input did Clara have on the subject? Clara wasn't my mom. On the other hand, if they ever played tug-of-war with me, if the school and Dr. Willner were dragging me off and my dad was pulling me back, I liked knowing that Clara would pitch in and put some extra weight on our side.

"Obviously," my dad said. "Meanwhile, stay clean, Tomster. Okay?"

"Don't call me that," I said. "And I *do* stay clean. I wish that staying clean was the answer."

Around that same time, I figured I'd keep my promise to Silas and go to the library and check out a book on Stalin. Of course, comparing our school to Stalinist Russia was just the sort of paranoid thinking Silas always used to indulge in. But now he no longer seemed paranoid. And besides, Stalin was interesting.

Going to the school library was faintly intimidating, mostly because I hardly ever went there. So I wasn't part of the inner circle, one of those people who knew the librarian, Mrs. Radacovich, on a first-name basis. Hi, Betty, hi, Bobby, hi, Susie. Hi there, Mrs. Rad. The fact that I went so rarely made me feel guilty about going at all, but I thought I might get extra credit for checking out a book that wasn't even required for class. Though I suppose I should have known better after my experience with *The Catcher in the Rye*.

I looked up Stalin on the computer catalog, and then in the old card catalog that Mrs. Rad still kept. But there was nothing between Stalactites and Stalagmites and States, United. See United States. Not exactly nothing. In the old catalog, there was a little fringe of torn paper still stuck there—as if something had been ripped out.

"Can I help you?" said Mrs. Rad.

I said, "Do you have any books on Stalin?"

The librarian jumped slightly. "Why, that's a peculiar request."

"Not really," I said. "I mean, isn't the guy one of the most important political figures of the century?"

"I suppose you could say that," said Mrs. Rad. "But we would never have anything like that in our library here at Central."

"Why not?" I said. "Isn't it history?"

"I guess so," said Mrs. Rad. "But it might upset the students."

Upset the students? When was *that* something the school worried about? And when was that the criteria for what they had or didn't have in the library? But if they were banning *The Catcher in the Rye* . . . well, Salinger seemed like nursery rhymes compared to the few facts I already knew about the life of Stalin.

"You can look on the shelves if you want," said Mrs. Rad. "In the biography section. But I'm sure we don't have anything like that."

She was just getting rid of me. But I checked the shelves anyway. There was an empty spot between a book on Scottish kings and another called *Stanley and Livingstone: Heroes of the African Continent*.

"Come back and see us again," said Mrs. Rad. She looked as if she were going to cry or as if there was something she wanted to say to me and couldn't.

That night I looked up Stalin on the Internet. I sat in the dark and shivered as I read how this one maniac from Georgia was personally responsible for the deaths of millions and millions of innocent people, including all the ones he sent off to labor camps to be rehabilitated and reeducated, except that education had nothing to do with it. They died there and never came back.

nine

THANKSGIVING CAME AND WENT, then Christmas. Holidays were always a little gloomy at our house since my mom died, even though the fact was, my mom hated holidays. She'd make the effort, she'd try her best, she'd cook some special dinner, but something inevitably went wrong. One Thanksgiving she forgot the pumpkin pie and filled the whole house with smoke. Another time she neglected to turn on the oven, and the Christmas turkey was raw. Always she'd sigh and shrug and say, "I don't know. I tried, I really did. I wanted you guys to have a nice holiday. I don't know what gets into me this time of year."

Actually it was confusing, because I *was* disappointed. I imagined that every other family was having the perfect meal, the perfect holiday. At the same time, my mom made it seem terrifically cool to just blow off the special festive dinner and leave the plates on the table and go out for burgers or pizza. And now it seemed pathetic that I had ever cared about anything as trivial as a pie or a turkey.

Poor Clara. It must have made her practically sick to roast a turkey, but she did. Crispy and juicy and golden brown, it looked like a turkey in a magazine, like a model turkey in an ad for perfect turkeys. My dad and I hardly touched it. Clara picked at the string beans.

For Christmas, my dad and Clara got me a set of night-vision goggles. The card said, "For Tom, our conspiracy theorist. With love." I'll admit that the goggles were sort of fun. I liked going out in the backyard and looking through them, even though it was already winter, even the raccoons were asleep, and there was hardly a squirrel to watch racing around in the darkness. Once I saw somebody's cat streaking through the woods behind our house. But the gift sort of annoyed me. Calling me their "conspiracy theorist" made everything I was worried about sound like a joke, like something invented by a kid trying to spook himself, when the fact was, Thanksgiving and Christmas passed, and there was still no sign of Silas. Every time we called his house, his mom said not to worry, she expected him home any day.

Basketball season started. We played some schools from around the state and from up in New Hampshire. Central High won a few, we lost a few. That is, the Dumb Jocks won some and lost some. Brian and Avery and I spent a lot of time on the bench, wishing Silas were still on the team.

Coach Pete kept giving us second chances, third and fourth and fifth chances, but we kept blowing it, committing fouls and missing easy shots. Our hearts just weren't in it. And the Dumb Jocks saw they'd been right about us all along. Why were we on the team anyway? To raise its grade point average?

After Christmas a couple of games were added

to our schedule, including one—a home game—against Pleasant Valley.

A day or so later Brian, Avery, and I were all called into Dr. Willner's office.

We got the notes in homeroom, so it wasn't until social studies that we realized that we were all supposed to go see Dr. Willner at the same time. We wondered what that could mean. We knew it couldn't be good. Was it because we were friends of Silas's? Or because there was something about our little clique in general and each of us in particular that Dr. Willner didn't like?

Avery said, "I'll bet we've broken some new rules we didn't even know about yet."

"Right," said Brian. "We're not allowed to breathe anymore. We're not allowed to go to the bathroom."

So it seemed pretty incredible when we finally got there and discovered that what Dr. Willner wanted to talk about was our highly embarrassing basketball season.

He said, "I gather that the three of you have been spending a good deal of time on the sidelines lately."

Nice of him to bring it up! We nodded miserably. There was no way to deny it. And what would be the point?

"And I'm sure you would probably prefer to participate more," said Dr. Willner.

"I guess that's Coach Pete's decision." Brian's voice had a razory edge, an unmistakable undertone of "mind your own business." That was so like Brian. He could say something that was, under the circumstances, brave and even confrontational, and just make it seem perfectly reasonable and straightforward.

Dr. Willner looked at him with hate. "It's the *school's* decision."

"It's not Coach Pete's fault," Avery argued, lawyerlike, as if Coach Pete were being accused. "Our game hasn't been exactly spectacular—"

"Hasn't gotten a *chance* to be spectacular. Or

even to improve," Dr. Willner said. "And I'm sure that you would like to get that chance and to play more. And we will personally see to it that you do, if you think you can do us . . . one little favor."

One little favor. When he said those three little words, we all caught our breath. I don't think we exhaled again until we were out of Dr. Willner's office.

"As you know, next week Central is playing Pleasant Valley. And after a meeting with my counterpart, the new grief and crisis counselor at Pleasant Valley High, we have decided that it would be nice if Pleasant Valley won."

"What?" we all said at once.

"We have decided that Pleasant Valley needs to feel good about itself. The team needs to be encouraged. After all, most of the Pleasant Valley players were not originally on the team, but courageously volunteered to fill in after so many of their classmates were killed. And quite a few of the players have been diagnosed with post-traumatic stress disorder. What that means is . . . well, it's something that happens to war veterans and victims of violent crimes."

I knew what post-traumatic stress disorder was. I'd seen a story on TV about a guy who claimed he had it and had literally gotten away with murdering his wife. I couldn't stand it when Dr. Willner talked down to us, as if we were idiots or small children.

He went on. "We can hardly imagine how much nerve it took for them to offer to substitute for the school heroes and victims whose lives were so cruelly, senselessly lost. But unfortunately the team has been defeated in almost every game they've played. And so we decided that it would be a healing experience for them to have a victory this time. Do you understand what I'm saying?"

Well, yes and no. We did, and we didn't. We knew what the words meant, but it didn't make any sense. We were supposed to let Pleasant Valley win *so they would feel good?* Still, one thing was clear enough: We were supposed to throw the game.

"It's come to our attention," Dr. Willner said, "that some of you have, at times, behaved as if you know better than the school administration. In regard to reading material, cell phones, and so forth." He was staring directly at me. "And we want you to know that if you continue to behave this way—let's say in regard to the game—there will be some serious and highly unpleasant consequences."

Consequences? What consequences? What did he have in mind? Would we be suspended or expelled? Or sent away, like Silas? And for what? For winning a basketball game?

In any case, we got the point: If we didn't do what Dr. Willner wanted, it was going to cost us. One way or another, he was going to make sure that we did what he said.

"So then. Is everything perfectly clear?"

We nodded and said nothing.

"Excellent, then," said Dr. Willner. "I'm looking forward to the game."

· · ·

It wasn't so much that we believed Silas about people reading our e-mails. But still we found ourselves avoiding the Internet over the next few days, and mostly talking to one another on the phone or, better yet, in person. We huddled together, nearly whispering, as we tried to puzzle out the mystery of what Dr. Willner was trying to do, and what *we* were going to do, and how we were going to do it.

Luckily, the late bus that took us home after practice was often slow in getting back from its early route, so we had a few minutes to stand outside, off to the side, on our own, talking in the cool fresh air. Even if they had the *trees* bugged, we weren't standing near enough to one so that anyone could hear us. How ironic that the only place we felt safe talking was the most open and obvious spot—right outside, in front of the school.

Almost as if we were the jury and Avery was delivering his closing argument, he paced the edge of the curb as he tossed the questions our way. "Willner wants us to throw the game so Pleasant Valley can feel *better*? What is *that* about? Does the dude have *money* on the game? That's the obvious line of reasoning. Follow the money. But somehow I think not. Nor, frankly, do I think the guy cares if Pleasant Valley feels better or not. Which leaves only one explanation."

Avery looked from me to Brian.

"I give up," I said.

"Because he *can*," said Brian. "Because he's got the power."

"Bingo," Avery said. "Because the dude *can* mess with us, he *will* mess with us. It's the law of the jungle. He just wants to make sure we know who's boss, and that he knows we know. That everybody knows the score."

"The guy just wants us to eat it," Brian said.

"Brilliant deduction," said Avery.

"But he's telling us to throw a game," I said. "Even if it *were* about being nice, that defeats the whole point of playing. We *can't* do it. We've got to do something. We need to tell someone. What about Coach Pete?"

"I don't think so," said Brian. "I don't think that Coach Pete wants us telling him this. It's way more information than he needs right now. Besides, he probably knows already."

"Anyway," I said. "What's the point of telling? Nobody will believe us."

"That's like a line from some horror B movie," said Avery.

"What is?" I said.

"*Nobody will believe us.*" Brian and I just stared at Avery. Somehow it sounded like something Silas would have said. His voice even sounded like Silas's. Then we all fell silent, and I knew—without having to ask—that all three of us were thinking about how Silas had made us watch *Invasion of the Body Snatchers*.

"Nobody *will*," said Brian at last. "Nobody *could* believe us. The whole thing's way too insane."

"What about our parents?" Brian and Avery looked at me. Was it because I'd said parents? Even *I* didn't know what I'd meant. Was I including Clara? Or did I mean *their* parents and my dad?

"If we tell our parents about this, it's Armageddon," said Brian. "Be prepared for full-scale parent-teacher war. I can see my mom really going into battle over this. Are we ready for that yet?"

Personally, I liked the thought of Brian's mom going to war with her sunglasses and leather jacket, going mano a mano against Dr. Willner. Intimidating him, I hoped. I would have paid money to watch it. At least *some* parent would be saying or doing something—and the good thing was, it wouldn't be *my* dad. I wouldn't have to deal with the consequences. Consequences. Dr. Willner had ruined the word. Just thinking it gave me the creeps.

"Not yet," said Avery. "It's not time for that yet. Let's save the big guns for when we need them. Let's see what we can work out on our own." He paused for a minute, thinking. "I don't know. It's weird. Every time I bring this stuff up with my mom and dad, it's like they're finding excuses for Dr. Willner and the school. They talk about how the school needs to protect us from what happened at Pleasant Valley. And of course, my dad's always pointing out how the school needs to protect *itself*. Liability. Whatever." I wasn't sure I agreed with Avery, but I decided to trust his judgment. Avery's dad was a lawyer. "And then they say that if we're not doing anything wrong, we haven't got anything to worry about." Avery paused. "Speaking of Silas . . ." No one *had* been speaking of Silas, though I guess we'd all been thinking about him.

"Speaking of Silas," repeated Avery, "I've got to say I'm a little surprised that he's the first one of us who got sent away."

"What do you mean?" I said.

"Usually," Avery said, "it's the black guy. Like

in the horror movies, you know? It's always the black guy who's the first to get chomped by the man-eating shark or zapped by the space alien or killed by the supergerm or whatever. So I always assumed that *I* would be the first to go. And I'm surprised that it was Silas."

"Dude, what are you talking about?" Brian said. The fact was, we often forgot that Avery was black until he brought it up. And it was always a little embarrassing when he did, when race came into the conversation. Besides, what did he mean by that "first to go" stuff? Silas got popped for smoking weed. Maybe Avery's parents were right: If we hadn't done anything wrong, we had nothing to worry about.

Except that it was no longer as simple as right and wrong. Now we had this little problem about the basketball game. Were we or were we not going to let Pleasant Valley win? Could we do it? How would that work? And what would happen to us if we didn't?

It was a hard decision to make on our own with no one to help us, nobody to bounce our ideas off— if we'd *had* any ideas. But beyond that, it almost felt as if we'd lost the power to make any decision at all. Now when my dad and I went to the diner and Nell asked, "Corn or green beans?" I could hardly answer. Sometimes in the morning I stood in front of the closet for a long time, trying to figure out what shirt to wear—even though my shirts were all pretty much the same. I couldn't decide what TV show to watch, what video game to play.

It was almost as if I didn't care, or as if everything were so much the same that it didn't matter. I remembered how that first night, after the shootings at Pleasant Valley, my dad had asked me if I was feeling especially stressed or anxious or sad. And I wasn't. Not then. Why would I have been? But now, as it turned out, I was. I was feeling all that and more.

As the days wore on, Brian and Avery and I couldn't even get ourselves to *talk* about the

Pleasant Valley game. The words just wouldn't come out. Not only didn't we know the answers—we couldn't ask the questions. I mean, we were *way* in denial. I kept trying to imagine how I would explain it to my dad. "Hey, Dad, like suppose you were about to play this basketball game, and someone . . . well, let's say your grief and crisis counselor, well, let's say someone asked you to throw the game and . . . so, like, what would you do?"

I think I just didn't want to put my dad to the test. On the one hand, I was scared that he might fail, that he might find some reason why it didn't *matter* if we won or lost, some reason why Dr. Willner had a point. On the other hand, I was even more worried that he would pass—that he would tell me we *had* to play as hard as we could, that we *had* to try and win. So that if we lost, no matter how hard we'd tried, my dad would never believe that I hadn't done it on purpose.

In any case, we did nothing and made no

decision at all until the day before the game. That afternoon, as we waited outside school for the late bus, Brian finally said, "I've figured it out. Let's just be normal."

"Normal? Define *normal*," Avery said.

"Normal," repeated Brian. "Normally we win sometimes, we lose sometimes. We do our best, but it doesn't always work. We'll just play completely normally and see what happens."

"But Pleasant Valley is a loser team," Avery pointed out. "*Everybody* wins against them."

"Then we win, and we'll deal with it," Brian said. "But meanwhile, we'll just be normal."

None of us had the faintest idea what normal could possibly mean under the circumstances. But it gave us a way to think and act, or maybe to not think and not act.

Nothing would change, we wouldn't do anything wrong. We wouldn't be brave or scared. We would just do whatever we had to do. We would just be normal.

• • •

But how could we have been normal—how could *anything* have been normal—after what happened during assembly on the morning of the game?

From the moment we filed in, we knew that something was different. But it took us a while to realize Mr. Trent wasn't there. Maybe the reason it took us so long to notice was that, over the past few months, our principal had gotten steadily quieter and more reserved. But lately he had seemed somehow smaller, as if he'd shrunk into himself, as if he'd curled up into a soggy little ball and was trying to disappear.

And now, finally, he *had* disappeared. Or at least he wasn't up on the auditorium stage with Dr. Willner. Had he been there yesterday? I suddenly couldn't remember.

Dr. Willner held up one hand, and the auditorium fell silent.

"First," he said, "it is my sad duty this morning

to inform you that our beloved principal, Mr. Trent, has decided to take early retirement and will not be with us any longer."

A gasp rose from the audience, mostly from the faculty section. They must have been thinking the same thing we were: Wasn't this awfully sudden? When someone was taking early retirement, wouldn't he announce it himself? And give a teary-eyed speech and say good-bye and get a big round of applause and maybe even a standing ovation? And wouldn't there be a Mr. Trent Appreciation Day, with a special assembly and teachers and students getting up to say what a great principal he'd been and how much we would miss him? When Mrs. Solomon retired last spring, we'd had something like that for her. And she was only the assistant *vice* principal. So why weren't we having an official good-bye appreciation day for Mr. Trent?

Avery said, "This is *really* weird. I'll bet you Willner killed him and dumped the body somewhere."

Brian said, "*My* bet is that Willner cut up Mr. Trent and stashed him in the freezer."

"Shut up, dudes," I said. Because they'd said it loud enough so that some girl was turning around in the row in front of us to see who had spoken. In the second or so till we figured out who it was, I gripped the arms of my seat.

Because we hadn't forgotten that e-mail advising parents to tell their kids to report any suspicious behavior. Someone had turned in Mrs. Ridley. And suggesting that Dr. Willner was a cold-blooded killer could have been considered suspicious behavior.

But the girl who had twisted around turned out to be Becca Sawyer. For a long time after the cell-phone incident that led to Mrs. Ridley's "health emergency," everyone assumed that Becca was dead meat. And yet for some reason they never punished her. For a few days, some kids had spread the rumor that Becca had been spared because she was a spy for Dr. Willner. But no one really believed it, and the rumor died away. I figured that the reason they let her go was sort of like the reason they were trying to make us throw the game—to show us that they could do what they wanted, when they wanted, how they wanted. They didn't have to follow the rules. They *made* the rules. They didn't have to be consistent.

Even though it was Brian and Avery who'd said that about Dr. Willner killing Mr. Trent, I was the one Becca looked at as she rolled her eyes and whispered, "*Really*."

For a moment it almost seemed possible that Becca liked me better than Brian. Up until then, I'd always taken it for granted that the very *definition* of a girl was, girls liked Brian better than me. And for a moment I almost wished that I'd been the one who'd joked—too loud—about Dr. Willner dismembering our former principal.

"I know you're as shocked and grief stricken as we are," Dr. Willner was saying. "But because Mr. Trent was the supremely caring, feeling, hard-working, humble man we all loved so much, he wanted to leave us with the minimum of fuss and the minimum attention focused on himself. So he has asked me to say his good-byes to you, and to share with you his warm best wishes for continued success in the future."

Dr. Willner paused, and we all applauded weakly. Was that what we were supposed to do? It seemed to be what was expected. As he waited for the applause to die out, our grief and crisis counselor nodded as if we were clapping for him.

And maybe he actually thought so, because the next thing he said was, "The district has formed a search committee to find and hire a new principal for Central. But in the meantime I have agreed to stay on and serve as your acting principal."

He stopped again, for more applause. But this time it was slower in coming. For a few moments no one could move, let alone bring their hands together energetically enough to produce an audible sound. What were we feeling? Fear, I guess. A certain dread, mixed with resignation. But the most unexpected emotion was a sharp and terrible pang of missing Mr. Trent. Why hadn't we appreciated him more? He'd been so easygoing. He'd asked nothing. He'd left us alone. He'd never tried to threaten or scare us, or make us fix a basketball game. He couldn't even remember our *names*. And we'd just dismissed him as some clueless nerd with no idea what was going on.

But it was hard to sort all this out, because my feelings about Mr. Trent were jumbled together with how much I missed Silas, and with how much I longed for the way our lives were before Pleasant Valley. Meanwhile, just thinking those two words—Pleasant Valley—sent chills down my spine. The basketball game was that night, and we still hadn't decided what to do except to try to be *normal*.

"On another front," Dr. Willner went on, "I have, as they say, some good news and some bad news." His smile made me think of a lizard, tracking a fat juicy fly. "First the good news. I'm extremely happy to report that two of our former students are making remarkable progress in Operation Turnaround."

Brian grabbed my shoulder, and Avery leaned over so his arm was touching mine. We knew he was talking about Silas, and I think we wanted to be in actual physical contact. But hadn't he just said two? Silas was the only one we knew about. Who else was there? "First of all, Jerry Gargiulo is excelling in Operation Turnaround's Maine program."

Jerry Gargiulo? Who was *he*? You could hear everyone asking their friends. No one seemed to have known him.

But maybe that was the point. Hadn't we been encouraged to report any friendless loners? Because wasn't that supposedly the story on the killers at Pleasant Valley? Nobody knew them, nobody paid any attention to them. That's why they went nuts and did it. Maybe poor Jerry Gargiulo was freezing his butt off in the snow up in Maine because he'd committed the new crime of not having any friends.

"Secondly," said Dr. Willner, and once more he seemed to be seeking us out of the entire auditorium and focusing on us, "Silas Archer is thriving at the Tucson camp."

Thriving? That didn't sound like Silas. But still, we were glad to hear news of him, even from Dr. Willner. It was great to hear someone say that Silas was doing okay. Because right around Christmas, when Brian had finally gotten up the nerve and called Silas's mom again, she said she hadn't talked to Silas in weeks. It seemed that kids were no longer allowed to call home from camp. Brian had said to Silas's mom, "I guess he'll be coming home soon." And Silas's mom had said, "Yes, dear, I'm sure he will."

"And finally," continued Dr. Willner, "the bad news." He paused, and you could see him adjusting his face, feature by feature, to look properly serious and solemn. "The bad news, which causes me great pain and sorrow to have to tell you, is that the third of our students, Stephanie Tyrone, was fatally injured in an accident while trying to escape from Operation Turnaround's western Nevada unit."

A gasp went through the auditorium, and some girls started sobbing, including a few who didn't even know Stephanie Tyrone. I had a terrible sinking feeling in the pit of my stomach. Stephanie Tyrone? How could she be dead? No one had ever said that *she'd* been sent to Operation Turnaround! The story was that she and her parents had moved to another town. And what had Stephanie done to deserve being shipped off to western Nevada? Worn a red ribbon that first day? Because they wanted to eliminate any possible troublemakers right at the very beginning? And now she'd been fatally injured in an *accident*? Who did they think would believe *that*? I was so sure that they'd killed her. All I could do was hope that something like that didn't happen to Silas. For a moment, I was scared I might start to cry right in the middle of assembly.

Dr. Willner shouldn't have told us about Stephanie. It was a major mistake on his part. We hadn't even known where she was. He didn't have to tell us. Even Stalin had lied about how many people he killed, how many he sent to the labor camps. But maybe Dr. Willner wanted us to be *exactly* as scared as we were when we found out what had really happened to Stephanie Tyrone. And maybe he wanted us to learn about it on the very morning of the day that Brian, Avery, and I were supposed to throw the game and let Pleasant Valley win.

He wanted us to know what the stakes were, and what was at risk. One slip, one mistake, one tiny hint of rebellion, and we could find ourselves in an even more terrible place, suffering the same fate that had happened to Stephanie, and maybe Silas, and that sorry loner, whoever he was, poor Jerry Gargiulo.

ten

THAT NIGHT MY DAD drove me to the game. Clara came along with us. Normally I didn't like her coming to our games because she always jumped up and screamed and yelled and attracted a lot of excessive attention. I imagined the other kids wondering what the point was, what was in it for her; she wasn't even my mom. But that night I was glad she was there. I needed all the support I could get. Having Clara on my side felt like reinforcements.

At dinner I couldn't eat. I kept saying, "No, thanks, I never eat before a game." Though the truth was, I always used to eat. Knowing that I had to play used to make me hungry.

Even though Avery and Brian and I had sworn not to tell anyone that Dr. Willner had ordered us to throw the game, I kept trying to think of a way to talk about some of the creepy stuff that was happening. I wanted to say something, I wanted to let my dad and Clara know just how much worse things at school were getting—or were about to get. But there wasn't time during dinner, or rather there wasn't a way to break into the conversation Dad was having with Clara. Both of them were complaining about their jobs, though in a joking way, so that you couldn't really tell if they were really complaining or just entertaining each other. First my dad described how his editor had called that day to complain that the Tuscan baked beans he'd drawn didn't look *Tuscan* enough. And then Clara told a story about a woman who'd come in to complain about a flowering cactus that she said was defective, and when Clara asked her how the cactus had gotten so soggy, the woman said she'd thought she was supposed to water it twice a day.

I was afraid it might spoil their fun if I brought up the fact that Dr. Willner had announced today that three kids from Central had been sent to Operation Turnaround, and that one of them was dead. But when we were in the car, going to the game, I decided to try.

It was always easier to talk to my dad in the car with both of us staring at the road and not having to look at each other, and it was even easier when I was in the backseat, in the dark. Clara had offered to ride in the back, but I said I preferred it, and that night I actually did.

No one had spoken for a while when I said, very casually, "Hey, Dad, did you hear that Mr. Trent quit?"

"Quit or retired?" my dad said. "The guy wasn't getting any younger."

"He wasn't that old," said Clara.

"I guess he took early retirement," I said. "That's what Dr. Willner told us."

"That explains it," said Dad.

"Dr. Willner," said Clara. "Gosh, that guy gives me the willies."

"The strange part was," I told them, "it was really sudden. I mean he was in school yesterday—I mean, I *think* he was in school yesterday, we'd all sort of stopped noticing—and today he just wasn't there. No good-byes, no Mr. Trent Appreciation Day, no speeches, no applause. The guy just disappeared."

"That *is* a little strange," said my dad. "But maybe they had some event just for the teachers, some ceremony or dinner or something, where they gave the guy the gold watch and had the speeches and—"

"The teachers didn't know about it," I said. "They found out when we did. Today. And they were just as surprised as we were. Doesn't that seem weird?"

"It does," said Clara. "It *does* seem strange."

"I guess it *does*," said my dad. "Everybody wants the gold watch. The reward for all those years of hard work and dependable service."

"But that's not the worst part. Today in assembly

Dr. Willner told us that three kids from Central have been sent to Operation Turnaround."

"Who besides Silas?" my dad said. "*Which* other two kids? Were they all doing drugs?"

I wish my dad hadn't said that.

"No," I said. "I'm pretty sure that this one girl, Stephanie Tyrone, got sent away for wearing this red AIDS ribbon she used to wear in memory of her brother."

"What was wrong with *that*?" Dad said.

"We're not allowed to wear red."

"You're not allowed to wear *red*?" Clara said. The light was finally dawning. Where had she been all these weeks when I'd been trying to tell them? "Why not?"

"That's what the killers at Pleasant Valley wore."

"I assume they wore shirts and jeans and sneakers," Clara said. "Are you allowed to wear shirts and jeans and sneakers?"

I laughed, and for just a minute I felt a little less

apprehensive. Maybe if Clara could joke around like that, things weren't as bad as we'd thought.

Then I said, "Wait. Listen. This isn't funny. Stephanie Tyrone's dead. They claim she got killed in an accident while she was trying to escape."

"Oh, my god," whispered Clara. And then no one said anything for quite a while.

Finally Clara said, "That's always happening at those terrible places. Every so often they go too far, and *Sixty Minutes* rushes out there with their cameras rolling, and then everyone just forgets about it until another kid gets hurt."

"What about the third kid?" asked my dad. "The third kid who got sent away."

"Nobody knew him. Nobody knew who he was. He was a total loner. Remember that e-mail they sent you saying we should report any kids whose behavior seemed suspicious? Everybody thinks that somebody reported him for not having any friends. His name was Jerry. Jerry Gargiulo."

"Nobody would do that," said my dad. "Turn another kid in for no reason except that he didn't have friends."

"I think it's happening, Dad," I said. "I have this sickening feeling about it."

"That *is* sickening," Clara said. "That is truly horrendous."

"I think there's worse stuff even than that going on," I said.

"What could be worse?" asked my dad. "Tom, what's going on at that place?"

This was the moment to tell them. And I almost did. But then something stopped me. It was almost as if I felt too sad. I thought of what might happen if Brian and Avery and I didn't do what Dr. Willner said. It occurred to me that I might wind up missing, like Silas . . . or Stephanie. And instead of feeling scared, the strange thing was, I felt sorry for my dad. I felt I had to protect him, which was strange, since he was always talking about protecting me. And school was always claiming that it was protecting *us*. Everything had gotten so confused, it was impossible to tell who was protecting whom—and from what.

"I don't know," I told him. And for a moment I didn't. Anyway, I decided I'd said enough for one night. We were almost at school.

We pulled into the parking lot at the exact same moment as the Pleasant Valley school bus. The whole length of the yellow bus was covered with a sign bordered with black and purple and lettered in big black block letters: WE WILL NEVER FORGET.

Well, of course they couldn't forget. The shootings were at their school. They actually knew the victims, the kids and teachers who were killed and injured. We weren't being allowed to forget for a minute, and it hadn't even happened to us.

My dad read the sign and said, "Why do I get the feeling this isn't going to be a fun game?"

"You don't know," I told him. "You don't know the half of it."

The door guards were at their usual stations, but they weren't seriously searching anyone. They were just giving everyone a quick visual once-over, checking a few kids' IDs. Bug Boy saw me, and I saw him. We pretended we'd never met.

The gym was full of students and parents. It was twice as crowded as usual. There must have been a special e-mail ordering everybody to come out. Or maybe everyone was just curious, eager to get a look at real live people from the school where the tragedy had happened.

My dad and Clara climbed up into the bleachers. I headed for the locker room. Brian and Avery were already there, together with most of the team. I was wearing my uniform under my clothes, which I shucked, then joined the others on the bench by the lockers.

Coach Pete looked stressed. That was not a good sign. What was he so disturbed about? For one thing, everyone knew that Pleasant Valley was a loser team. For another, even in the best of times, he'd never seemed to take it personally whether we won or lost. Though, in fact, he'd cared a lot. But lately he'd stopped caring, or concentrating, or something, which was another reason why we hadn't exactly had the most slamming season so far.

Then I thought that maybe he was physically uncomfortable, because he was wearing a suit and a tie, though for games he generally wore some kind of Mr. Rogers grandpa-type sweater.

Coach Pete said, "As you guys all know, this isn't an ordinary game. These guys have been through hell. Their friends are dead. They're still healing. And this isn't the original team." He paused and cleared his throat. "As you guys all know. Still, we've got to be normal. Regular. We play to win. But we don't want this to be a—"

He closed his eyes and shook his head. "I almost said massacre. Jeez."

Everybody laughed, or tried to laugh. That's how edgy we were. A few Dumb Jocks *did* laugh, and everybody turned to glare at them as if they were criminals.

"In any case," said Coach Pete. "It isn't much of a challenge. So I figured we'd give some of you second-string guys a chance to start, for a change."

I wished he hadn't said that. It gave me a definite feeling that Coach Pete had also had a conversation with Dr. Willner about tonight's game, about the importance—the necessity!—of making the Pleasant Valley team feel better. Maybe he was worried that if he sent the usual starters in first, they'd rack up such a lead that Pleasant Valley could never catch up and get to feel good about themselves. Though possibly I was imagining this. Maybe Coach Pete was just doing what he said he was doing: giving us a chance to start in a game we could win, no matter what.

In any case, I was willing to bet that Coach Pete knew a lot more than we did about what was going on at Central. What had happened to Mrs. Ridley and Mr. Trent and Silas and the others.

Maybe all the faculty had found out the truth, or suspected. And maybe Coach Pete knew the most of all. His wife worked for Dr. Willner.

"What's this about? What for? I don't get it," said one of the Dumb Jocks. "Since when do those guys get to start?"

"Since I decided," Coach Pete told them. "All right, Brian, you're playing center. And Avery, man, you take small forward. And Tom, you're point guard."

Nothing was normal, obviously. Lately, the few times we had gotten to play, Avery had played point guard.

"Okay?" said Coach Pete. "Everyone understand?"

Actually, it was not okay. It was totally *not* okay. I suddenly forgot about all those games when I'd sat on the sidelines wishing I was the point guard because I could have done a better job at calling the plays and figuring out what the other team's strengths were, reading the defense and deciding what needed to be done.

Two of the regular starters—a guy named Jeff and our captain, Jaycee—would be taking their usual positions.

Coach Pete wrote our names on the blackboard and assigned us to the guys we were supposed to guard, man to man. I was supposed to take this tall redheaded kid. Coach Pete said, "You can't miss the guy. He'll be easy to keep your eye on." He ran through the offense strategy that we would be playing, three guys along the three-point line, the other two in constant motion looking for an opening.

"Keep awake, keep moving, keep looking for the ball, run the baselines, know where your teammates are at every moment." He motioned for us to huddle. We piled our hands together. In the middle of the huddle, I searched for Brian and Avery. I wondered what they were thinking. How were we going to do this?

But both of them were focused on the pile of

hands. We lifted our arms and said, "Team!"

Out on the court, the Pleasant Valley team was already doing layups. One look and we could tell that Coach Pete—and Dr. Willner—hadn't been exaggerating. It wasn't just that the players were missing nearly every shot. It was the totally tragic vibe you could feel from clear across the gym.

Brian came over to me and whispered, "*Major* post-traumatic stress disorder."

I said, "Have you seen Willner? Where's he sitting?"

Brian gestured toward the bleachers. Dr. Willner was in the very front row, next to his tiny mouse-wife. I wished Brian hadn't pointed at him, because he caught us looking and nodded at us, and a whole flock of butterflies began tearing around in my stomach.

The buzzer sounded. Jaycee and the Pleasant Valley captain shook hands with the referee and with each other. The redheaded point guard *was* easy to find. I went over and stood near him.

"Hey," he said.

"Hiya," I said.

His face had the strangest expression. Terrified, I would have said. As if I were going to hit him. Then it struck me that maybe he saw it, maybe he saw the Pleasant Valley students get killed. And he couldn't forget it, he *couldn't* get over it, he kept thinking it was going to happen again, that some normal, apparently ordinary kid—like me— might suddenly pull out a gun and start shooting. I wanted to say something, to tell him that I was sorry about what happened at his school, to promise that I wasn't going to hurt him. But I couldn't think of anything to say that wouldn't make things worse, or wouldn't sound completely embarrassing and stupid.

So I just shut up and watched as Brian and the tallest kid on the Pleasant Valley team got ready to jump for the ball. What else could I have done? I kept one eye on the redheaded kid and pretended that everything was normal.

A couple of minutes into the game, Brian ran up the court, close enough to hiss at me, "Trust me, dude. I've got a plan."

I thought: Excuse me, *I'm* the point guard! We were supposed to follow *my* plan! This might be the only chance I ever got to have a plan of my own! The only problem was that I didn't have a plan, except Brian's plan: Be normal.

Then I spotted Dr. Willner again, out of the corner of my eye. And I realized that *he* had a plan, and if he carried out *his* plan, I would definitely never get another chance to have anything like a game plan.

So I tried to figure out what Brian's plan could be. I studied him as closely as I could, without taking my eye off the other team, which turned out to be easy. That's how slow they were.

And after a while, I understood what Brian had in mind. When, and only when, the other team scored a basket, which wasn't very often, then Brian would start to hustle, and we would tie the score, and then slack off and hang back until they scored again.

I thought, How totally brilliant! We could always tell Dr. Willner that we thought a tie would be good enough. Pleasant Valley didn't have to actually *win*. Given their record so far, they would feel better about themselves if they just didn't get slaughtered. We wouldn't say "get slaughtered." We could say we thought that was what Dr. Willner meant, that we'd misunderstood and thought that a dead heat would be fine. And maybe that would work and at least give us some time to recoup and get ourselves together until he gave us the next impossible order that he would insist we carry out.

Needless to say, it was a crazy game. Mostly we concentrated on defense, making sure that the other team didn't score. Then when they got a basket, we played catch-up, but just enough so that we didn't pull out more than two points ahead, and then we went back on defense again. It gave the game a strange rhythm, but it seemed to be working. The best part was that we were still being spared from having to make a decision. We weren't letting them win, we weren't *not* letting them win. We weren't winning. We were just keeping things cool, keeping everything even.

It was hard to tell if the crowd knew that something wasn't right. On the one hand, it was sort of an exciting game, because the score was always close, or tied. On the other hand, it must have been clear that no one was playing too well or too hard. The crowd cheered, and then they stopped cheering. Then they cheered again.

I had the definite feeling that the redheaded guy I was guarding knew that something was fishy. He kept giving me these curious, pathetic looks, and the funny thing was, it made me mad. It was almost as if I thought the whole thing was *his* fault, though of course I really didn't. I knew that the killers at Pleasant Valley were dead, and that I was supposed to feel sorry for the survivors.

And I did, I felt sorry for them. But still I was angry that it had happened and changed my life.

Even the cheerleaders seemed bewildered. They kept screwing up their routines, turning in the wrong direction, getting way out of synch, even though they normally had every step and every move clockwork perfect. Meanwhile I was being very careful not to glance in Dr. Willner's direction. Because if what we were doing wasn't good enough for him, I didn't want to know about it.

The other guys on our team didn't understand what was happening at all. At the end of the quarters and at halftime they were all over Coach Pete, demanding to know what was going on, why they weren't playing. Why couldn't we pull out further ahead and just nail the game?

Coach Pete kept saying that he didn't want to mess up a good thing, that the team was doing well—or well enough. So why change the lineup and spoil it? None of it made any sense. For one thing, we weren't doing *that* well, the score was low, we were tied. If we'd wanted to, we could have creamed the Pleasant Valley team in two seconds. Besides which, it was unheard-of not to rotate the players, even once in a game. The only reasonable explanation was that Coach Pete had gotten the same orders we had. So he must have been relieved that we were finessing the situation for him.

Maybe the fact that it *was* all so strange worked in Coach Pete's favor. Even the dumbest of the Dumb Jocks knew that something highly unusual was happening, and because they couldn't figure it out at *all*, they just sat back and let it happen.

It seemed to be working, and it *would* have worked if luck hadn't turned against us. Everything would have been fine if I hadn't been forced to make the decision that we'd all been trying not to make ever since the day that Dr. Willner called the three of us into his office.

Two minutes before the end of the game, Avery fouled the guy he was guarding. The kid missed the first shot, which was no big surprise.

And then he made the second one.

The score was 47 to 46. Pleasant Valley was one point ahead. What were we supposed to do now? I assumed that the answer was what Brian had said: Try and make everything be normal. Or at least *seem* normal. Did we really want them to win? A tie had been okay. But I still couldn't quite get my head around actually losing.

I caught a pass from Avery and started dribbling down the court, not pressing too hard, not slowing up, just sort of taking my time. If the buzzer rang before I could shoot, that would be fine with me. Or almost fine, because already something was kicking in, some unhelpful jolt of honesty and way more integrity than I needed at that particular moment.

I'd pulled out in front of everyone else. I had the court to myself. The basket was up in front of me. I knew I could make the shot if I wanted. All I had to do was take my time, aim, remember everything Coach Pete had told us back in those long-lost, faraway days when our minds and hearts were clear, when we still wanted to win. Back in that simple, innocent time. Before Pleasant Valley.

All at once I felt something slam into me. I lost my balance. I was falling. The gym floor came up to meet me. Suddenly I was lying on my back staring up at the ceiling and then at the faces coming into focus, one by one, looking down at me. I remember thinking how worried they looked, and that they shouldn't have been so alarmed, because the real danger had nothing to do with whether I was injured. The real question was: What would happen now—and after the game was over? But that wasn't what they were asking me. "Are you hurt? Are you okay?" How could I have answered them? I didn't have the faintest idea.

"Are you okay?" said Coach Pete.

"I think so," I said weakly.

The face of the redheaded kid slowly swam into focus. "Hey, man, I'm sorry," he said. Only then did I realize what had happened. He had fouled me as I was taking a shot.

All my body parts seemed to be movable. And in fact, nothing hurt too badly, though one of my knees and my elbow felt bruised. So I knew this was just a taste of how much it was going to hurt later. But for now there was no reason to keep lying on the floor, though the truth was, I sort of liked it. It was restful and easy, a moment out of time, delaying what was about to happen next.

"Foul!" said the referee. And now I really wished I could have kept lying there. Because I was starting to do the math and to understand what I was facing.

One shot would tie the game. The second would win it. So here it was—the moment of truth. The moment I'd been dreading.

I stood up. The crowd roared.

The referee tossed me the ball. I moved slowly—more slowly than I needed to—toward the foul line. Because what I really needed was time, all the time I could get.

Okay. Fine. I took a deep breath. The first shot was not the problem. Even if I made it, it would still only mean that the game would be tied. And maybe I would blow it, even if I tried my hardest. I'd missed a million shots in my life. All I had to do was miss one more—that would solve all my problems.

I aimed and shot. The ball swished through the net. The bleachers erupted in cheers. Normally I would have looked at the crowd, trying to pick out my dad and Clara. Was Becca Sawyer there tonight? I would have liked to see her. But I didn't want to check out the crowd. I was afraid that my gaze would stray, and that I'd find myself locking eyes with Dr. Willner. Which would just make everything way more complicated, and harder.

I spun the ball between my hands. Then I spun it again. How many seconds could you take out here before it started seeming weird? But how could I rush something like this when so much depended on it? For example, my life. Was I being melodramatic? What scared me was, I didn't think so. Dr. Willner meant business. Silas and two other kids were gone. Stephanie was dead. And maybe there were others, more loners like Jerry Gargiulo, kids who Dr. Willner hadn't even bothered to mention.

I looked up at the basket. My legs felt shaky. I flexed my knees a few times.

I wasn't great at foul shots anyway. I could always miss, regardless. I certainly had before. But suddenly I was bizarrely sure that I could *choose* to make it or to miss, whichever I wanted. Suddenly I *had* to decide, and at that same moment it struck me that there *was* no decision. I couldn't lose on purpose. Throwing the game was wrong. Cowardice was wrong. And the worst thing would be to throw the game because I was scared of Dr. Willner. I knew that if we won, I would live to regret it. That there would be times when I would wish with all my heart that I had listened to Dr. Willner, and lost.

The gym was totally silent. It was almost as if the crowd knew what was at stake. But of course they couldn't have known, except for Brian, Avery, Coach Pete. And, of course, Dr. Willner.

I raised the ball and arced it toward the net. There was never the slightest doubt as to where it was headed.

Swish.

The crowd went insane.

And the buzzer sounded at just that very second.

"Central! Central!" everyone yelled. And then they were chanting my name. "Bishop! Bishop!" But the only word I was hearing was *consequences.*

The guys on my team ran out on the court, and everyone was hugging and slapping one another on the back. Even Brian and Avery, who really should have known better. The good news was that we'd won the game. The bad news was that we were toast.

But my friends forgot that, they forgot themselves, they even forgot Dr. Willner. For a few minutes, they even forgot how much had changed since Pleasant Valley. They were happy, like they used to be, just because we'd won the game. The reality would hit them soon enough. I didn't have to set them straight.

Only I couldn't forget Dr. Willner. I was the one who had made the shot.

The crowd was hustling down onto the court. I saw Dad and Clara running toward me, waving and grinning. But Dr. Willner didn't move, and I could see his head above the heads of the kids and parents streaming around him. It was like a disembodied head, floating above the crowd, like a hologram of a head, Dr. Willner's head, and the head located me at the exact same instant that I found it. Dr. Willner looked at me, and I *knew* I hadn't been wrong about how bad things were, and what might happen now.

Coach Pete knew I was a dead man. I could tell it from his face when I passed him on the way to the lockers, and he punched me lightly on the arm.

"Good game, man," he said. Maybe we were both dead. I had no idea what Dr. Willner had said to Coach Pete, or what the coach had riding on this. It showed what a good guy Coach Pete was that he'd said nothing about it, one way or the other. He hadn't told us to lose or to make Pleasant Valley feel better, even though his job—and for all I knew, his life—might be depending on it. He'd done the legal, acceptable limit of what could be done to sabotage the game. He'd let the second string start and play the whole time. But even that hadn't been enough.

I got dressed and was out of there before the other guys came in to change into their street clothes. I couldn't deal with their happiness, or with wondering exactly how long the grim reality would take to dawn on Brian and Avery.

My dad and Clara would be waiting for me. They'd been the first down on the court, hugging me, telling me how well I played, what a hero I was. And it made me feel guilty, even though I knew I'd basically done the right thing.

Because if anything happened to me, it would really hurt my dad. And *he* hadn't gotten to choose. It had been entirely my decision. I told myself that my dad would have done exactly the same thing that I did.

Thinking about my dad and Clara made me want to go home.

As I hurried out of the locker room, I noticed some guy lurking outside. By then I was so jumpy that for a second I imagined that it was some psycho prison guard Dr. Willner had sent to drag me off immediately to the Antarctica outpost of Operation Turnaround. Or to kill me, like they'd murdered Stephanie, and say I'd died trying to escape. But there probably would have been two of them, and they would have been bigger.

It took me a few seconds to recognize the red-headed guy from Pleasant Valley. I was so glad that it was him I burst into weird laughter. Maybe he thought I was laughing at him. He seemed even sadder and more haunted than he had on the court.

"Can I talk to you a minute?" he said.

What did he want to tell me? Did he want to apologize, to say he was sorry he'd fouled me? The truth was, I should have thanked him for that. It was the reason we'd won. Or did he want to say something else . . . something about Pleasant Valley?

Half of me was curious. Half of me didn't want to hear it. I knew that this guy was completely not at fault for what had happened at his school. He was the victim. He hadn't done it, he couldn't help it, he'd been hurt worse than anyone except the kids and the families of the kids and teachers who'd been injured or killed. And I knew that it was wrong of me to resent him. But that was how I felt—annoyed at anyone who was even connected to Pleasant Valley. I was glad we'd won the game.

"Sorry," I said. "Gotta run." And I left him standing at the locker-room door, like some groupie waiting for the team to come out so she could ask for their autographs.

I was heading for the door nearest the parking lot where I was supposed to meet Dad and Clara. Just as I was leaving school, someone grabbed my arm. If it turned out to be the redheaded kid, I was going to haul off and slug him.

I wheeled around. It was Becca. And it completely surprised me, how happy I was to see her. It wasn't as if we were such great friends, but at that moment she was the person in the whole world I most . . . well, let's just say I was glad she was there. I grinned. I couldn't help it.

I said, "What are you *doing* here?"

"Uh," she said. "I was at the game."

"Obviously," I said.

"You were great," she said. "You were beautiful."

"So great that I'm dead," I said.

"What do you mean?" said Becca. "Dead, like, dead tired?"

"Dead like in the ground," I said. For some reason, I didn't hesitate. The truth came pouring out. "Willner told me to throw the game."

"Are you serious?" Becca said.

"Totally," I said.

"Do you want to talk?" Becca said.

"Definitely," I heard myself say. I *think* it was my voice. It sounded like someone else. "But where? My dad's out there waiting for me so he can drive me home."

"We can walk to my house from here. My dad's away on business. But my mom can drive you home." I could have sworn that Becca was just as surprised as I was to find herself saying something she wouldn't normally have said.

"Are you sure she'll want to do that?" I said.

"My mom's cool," said Becca.

Becca came with me to find my dad. It felt like being a child again, and ambushing your parents with some scheme about a play date you cooked up with your friends that your mom and dad weren't expecting.

I explained to my dad as best as I could. The whole situation was highly embarrassing. But I seemed to be lucking out. Dad got it immediately. He didn't ask any questions, or make any jokes, which would have made it even more humiliating.

In general, my dad was always trying to find out if I had a girlfriend, but he couldn't bring himself to ask directly about something he knew was private. So he'd usually say something lame like, "What are the girls in your class like?" And I'd say, "Mostly stupid," and we'd let it go at that.

Now he thought he'd found out, and it annoyed me that he was jumping to conclusions. Because this wasn't like that at all. Becca and I were just friends.

My dad asked Becca if she was sure it would be okay with her mom to drive me home, and when Becca said yes, my dad said, "Okay, Tom, but remember. I expect you back by ten. It's a school night, remember? Do you guys want a ride to Becca's house? Clara and I can drop you off." At least he hadn't called me Tomster.

"No, thanks. We can walk," I said.

Then Dad said to Becca, "Didn't Tom play great tonight?" I should have known. He would do *something* embarrassing.

"Totally amazing," Becca said.

Then we all just froze until finally I said, "Okay. Bye."

"Have fun," Clara called from inside the car.

"Thanks," I said. "See you later."

"Ten at the latest. Promise," said my dad.

"I promise," I said, and we left.

The night was chilly, but I didn't feel cold as we headed up the road behind the football field and up the hill above school to the neighborhood of small, modern houses where Becca lived. My hair was still wet from the game. I wished I had taken a shower. Maybe I would get a cold, which would be okay with me. If I missed a few days of school, it would give me that much more slack till I had to go deal with Dr. Willner.

We walked for a while without talking. Then, as if she were reading my mind, Becca said, "So what was it you were saying before—you know, about Dr. Willner?"

"Nothing, really," I said. "I don't know what I was saying. I—I made that up." Becca looked at me strangely. "Okay, sure, whatever," she said.

I would have loved to tell her the whole story, to make myself seem like a hero, a guy so brave and honest that he couldn't throw a game even though he'd been threatened and browbeaten and basically told that his life might be at stake. On the other hand—I was thinking fast—it was information she didn't need. If things got really ugly, Becca didn't have to know that the grief and crisis counselor, our acting principal, had tried to bully and threaten us into letting Pleasant Valley win the game.

We walked along the edge of the road in the darkness. A few times Becca stumbled and almost fell in my direction. I reached out my hand to catch her. On both sides of the road were neat houses, garages, driveways, mailboxes. Beyond the windows, I could see the flickering lights of TVs. I wondered if any of these people peacefully watching the tube had kids at Central, and if any of them knew what was going on.

Finally Becca said, "Listen, did you ever hear anything about what happened to Mrs. Ridley?"

"You mean like where she went to?"

"Yeah."

"Only what they told us. That health emergency story."

"And did you believe that?"

"Not really," I said.

"Me neither," Becca said. "Plus I felt totally guilty. Because it was *my* cell phone that rang and that must have gotten her into trouble."

"It wasn't your fault," I said. "*You* didn't know it was going to ring in her class."

Becca said, "I knew I should have left my phone home. I knew what the new rule was. But the whole thing made me so mad. It was like I wasn't in control. I just sort of forgot to take it out of my backpack. And that morning—for the first time practically *ever*—nobody searched my backpack."

"I know what you mean about not being in control," I said. I was thinking about that foul shot. Suddenly I was terrified, and I didn't want to feel that way around Becca.

"For about a week after that, I couldn't sleep at night. I could hardly eat. I kept thinking I was about to get into horrible trouble. But it was so mysterious. . . . I mean, the fact that nothing bad happened to me. I never heard a word about the phone. No one ever mentioned it."

A couple of thoughts flashed through my mind. First, it was so obvious that Becca was the last person in the school who would have spied for Dr. Willner. And second . . . I thought, well, just maybe, if Becca hadn't gotten into trouble about the phone, it was possible, remotely possible, that I wouldn't get into trouble about the game. Though I knew that was probably too much to hope for.

"I guess you dodged a bullet," I said.

After another silence she said, "Hasn't school been weird lately?"

"That's an understatement," I said, and I laughed. Not because anything was funny. But because it was comforting to be having this conversation. It was as if everybody—or at least someone else—knew what was happening at Central. Until then, it had seemed like Brian and Avery and I were the only ones who'd noticed what was going on. And also, once upon a time, Silas.

"I've been really scared," she said. "That was so terrible about Stephanie Tyrone. And about Silas getting sent away. I know he was your friend."

There was a very long silence. Then I said, "Be afraid. Be very afraid." And then we laughed again.

"Have you told your mom?" I asked.

"Yeah, she's totally on my side. But I think she's confused. She doesn't know what to do. She's kind of holding her breath and waiting, like everyone else, to see what happens next."

"My dad, too," I said. "I mean, he's on my side.

And also clueless. I think Brian's mom might do something. Go to the school board, maybe."

"That would be good," said Becca. Then she said, "Hey, does your dad read the e-mails they send home from school?"

"Sometimes," I said. "I guess so. Why do you ask?"

"Because I have this strange feeling that they're using them to . . . I don't know . . . brainwash the parents. A couple of my friends have told me that their parents have started acting like robots. Whenever they try to talk to their parents, all their moms and dads do is repeat the stuff they've read in the school e-mails. And their parents are acting weird. They're not listening, they're always saying that school is right, no matter what happens."

"I'm not sure," I said. "I know my dad *was* reading them." Suddenly I had this fluttery feeling down in the pit of my stomach. And for some reason I remembered how I felt when my mom was in the hospital after the accident, and I woke up in the morning, and I knew that my dad was about to tell me that she'd died during the night.

"Just as long as he stops reading them," Becca said. "Because I think the brainwashing takes a while to kick in, it doesn't happen right away."

"Silas's mom . . ."

"What about her?" said Becca.

I recalled the way Silas's mom had kept talking about the e-mails from school. But it was just too painful to talk about Silas right then.

The silence felt like pressure now. There was something I wanted to say. The thought of how I'd feel later if I didn't say it seemed worse than my fear of being embarrassed if I said it now.

"You know what I can't help wishing?" I asked.

"That Pleasant Valley never happened," said Becca.

"Sure, that," I said. "But besides that. I wish my mom was still alive. She always knew what to do about even the stupidest little problem. I would tell her what it was, what was bothering me, and she would figure it out. She would get this funny distant look on her face and start twirling a strand of her hair like a little kid, and she would think so long that I almost began to worry she'd forgotten all about it. And then she'd come back from wherever she was with the perfect solution." What I couldn't bring myself to say was this: The truth was, what made me saddest was that I was already forgetting my mom. There were some things I knew she'd said and done. But they were becoming just stories I told myself, like the stories I remembered—or told myself—about when I was a child.

"Hey, are you okay?" Becca asked.

"Yeah," I said. "I'm fine."

"Do you think your mom would have known what to do about *this*?" Becca said.

"About what?" I said.

"You know. About what's been happening at school? And about Dr. Willner?"

I almost reached out and put my finger on her

lips, that's how careful I'd gotten, talking with Brian and Avery, thinking everywhere was bugged. But if we were bugged now, the world was bugged. And there was no hope. There was nothing we could do. Plus, just her saying Dr. Willner's name had brought everything back—the game, and what I'd done, and what I might be facing. It was strange that I'd been able to put it out of my mind, even for a second. It was like right after my mom died, I'd have these little moments of forgetting, and then I'd remember and feel much worse than I had before.

"I don't know," I said. "I really don't. This is pretty tough." *Would* my mom have known what to do?

It almost didn't matter. It felt so good to talk about her. There were other things I wished I could say. Like about how sometimes when my dad was driving and my mom was riding shotgun, she'd reach behind her, back around her seat, and grab my hand and give it a squeeze. And about how when she died, I realized that no one would do that for me again. Ever. The truth was, I didn't *want* anyone to do it. I would hate it if Clara even tried. But I didn't tell any of this to Becca. I'd said enough for now. It felt great just to talk about how my mom twirled her hair when she was trying to figure something out.

"I heard about your mom," Becca said. "I'm sorry. You were like in sixth grade, right? That must have been really hard."

"That's okay," I said.

"Actually, I was thinking about all that earlier tonight," Becca said.

"You were?" I said.

"I was thinking about Stephanie Tyrone, and how having had something really tragic happen in her life had made her braver than anyone else. So she was the first one who stood up to Dr. Willner—and the first one who got sent away. And the first one who got killed. Don't you think that's what happened? Don't you think she was killed?"

"I do," I said. "And now I'm scared that might happen to Silas." And then suddenly I couldn't breathe. I had to bend over and catch my breath.

"Are you *sure* you're okay?" asked Becca.

"Yeah, I'm fine. I just got a weird cramp."

"Anyway, tonight I was thinking that about *you*. I mean, it was really brave of you to make that shot and win the game."

"What do you mean?" I said warily.

"Because you were supposed to lose."

"I told you . . ." I said. "I made that stuff up, I— I wish I never mentioned it."

"Don't worry. I knew before you told me," she said. "Or anyway, I suspected. I knew that something was really weird. Coach Pete kept the second string in all game. What was *that* about? I mean, that *never* happens. The thing that I found really odd was—didn't anyone notice?"

"I wondered about that," I told her. "About why no one noticed." I liked it that Becca's being smart went way beyond getting good grades. I felt as if the fact that she was here with me meant that I was smart, too, though I'd hardly ever thought of myself that way. Maybe I was more intelligent than I'd thought. And though I liked it that Becca thought I was brave, it made me feel worse than ever that she was grouping me along with Stephanie and Silas. It wasn't what I wanted to hear. I knew that Stephanie Tyrone had been beautiful and courageous. But still, it wasn't exactly a clique I wanted to belong to.

"I think we'd better change the subject," I said. "This is starting to freak me out."

We'd gotten to her house. As we walked up to the front door, I felt a kind of panic, and before we got to the steps, I grabbed her shoulders and turned her toward me and kissed her. In the beginning, I missed her mouth, though not by very much. And after a few tries, I found it.

I didn't have to think about it. It was a little like making the foul shot earlier in the evening. My body—or something—just did it. I had no idea what I was doing. Becca tensed up, then she kissed me back. Her lips were soft and tasted like the cold air.

After a while we stopped and went inside. Becca's mom was friendly. We all sat in the living room. It was totally awkward. It would have felt way too uncomfortable to go off to her room to play video games or pretend to study, the way I might have done at another guy's house. I knew it was retarded to feel like that. All we'd done was kiss. Plenty of guys my age had had sex already. Brian, for example. And so we just sat there. Becca's mom brought me a can of soda. I liked it that she didn't bother bringing me a glass or asking if I wanted one, which would have been more momlike. Not asking was something my mom would have done.

We sat in Becca's living room. Becca's mother kept coming up with polite questions. Which of Becca's classes are you in? Are you in chorus, too? She was really working hard. Finally I said I had to go. It was a school night. I had homework.

"Hear that, Becca?" said her mom. As if Becca had ever in her *life* needed someone else to remind her to do her homework. "Why don't you stay home and start yours, and I'll give Todd a ride home."

"Tom," Becca said. "His name is Tom. Mom. My god—"

"Be polite, hon," said Becca's mom. "Let's see how many names you get right when you're my age."

Becca's mom drove me home in their noisy, five-year-old Saab. Except for when I had to give her directions, we didn't talk, which was fine. I actually felt pretty comfortable, as if we'd known each other for years. I thanked her and got out. It was way before ten.

My dad and Clara were watching TV in the living room.

"Hey, Tomster," said Dad. "Want to watch with us? Or do you have homework?"

"Don't call me that," I said.

All of a sudden I had that sinking feeling again—something's wrong!—long before I knew why. Then I remembered: Dr. Willner. How grief stricken my dad would be if I got sent away, like Silas. First my mom, and now me. I wanted to watch TV with them, but the whole thing—just being with them—suddenly seemed way too sad. I imagined my dad and Clara, after I got killed, like Stephanie, watching TV to take their minds off how much they missed me. Half of me wanted to burst into tears and beg them to help me, get me out of there, do something before Dr. Willner sent me to Operation Turnaround and they never saw me again. I knew my dad would help me if it came down to that, I remembered how contemptuously he'd talked about Silas's parents. And it made me feel better or, anyway, slightly less scared. So why didn't I say anything? Because, I guess, the other half of me—the half that won out—still wanted to believe that everything was okay: that Silas was coming home, that Stephanie's death was an accident, and that the consequences Dr. Willner had threatened me with were, like, a week of detention.

"That's okay, I've got homework," I said. "Maybe I'll come out and hang with you guys later."

My dad yelled after me, "Oh, Avery called. He said call him, no matter how late."

Then I said, very casually, "Hey, Dad, by the way was there any e-mail from school? Anything I should know about?"

I held my breath until my dad said, "Gee, Tomster, I don't know. The truth is, I've stopped reading them. They take so much time, and they're so long and depressing. The *real* truth is, I've started deleting them before I even read them. But if you need me to start reading them again, I will." My dad sounded guilty, as if he thought that his not keeping up with the school e-mail meant that he was a bad, irresponsible parent. There was no way to tell him how happy and relieved I was to hear it.

"No," I said. "I think you're right. It's probably a bad idea to waste your time on stuff that, I promise you, we hear fifty times a day at school. So, uh, good night, Dad. Love you."

"Love you, too," said Dad.

"Good night, Clara," I said.

"Good night, Tom," said Clara.

I went to my room. There was e-mail on my computer. Three messages from Avery saying I should get in touch with him immediately. Whenever. Red alert.

I figured it couldn't be about the basketball game, or about what I thought Willner was going to do to us now that we'd won. The three of us had gotten careful about the e-mail and the phone. I decided that it was about Becca, that someone had seen me leaving school with her and told Brian and Avery, and now Avery was trying to find out what had happened.

I didn't want to go into it. I decided to ignore

Avery's messages. I'd talk to him in the morning. That would be soon enough.

Later, of course, I wished that I'd talked to him that night. Though maybe it wouldn't have changed anything—just the details of how it happened.

eleven

T HE NEXT MORNING, as soon as I got on the bus, I could see that Avery looked totally crazed. Brian just seemed worried. Both gazed emptily at the TV, but neither was watching. Or talking.

When I got on, Brian said to me, "I can't believe we won. I mean, that you made that foul shot. We are in *so* much trouble. Dude, how smart was that? Was that about being a hero? A sports star? Michael freaking Jordan? Because maybe you should have consulted *us*—"

"Forget about that," said Avery. "That is not the weird part."

"Oh, right," said Brian. "Avery's got some stuff to tell us that he refused to get into before you got on the bus."

Avery said, "I've been waiting for you, man,

because I've got the strangest—I mean the scariest—stuff to say that you have ever heard in your entire life. Are your ready for this?"

I was glad that whatever Avery had to say was about to take the heat off me and postpone the discussion of what Dr. Willner was going to do now that we'd defied his orders and won the basketball game. That is, *I'd* defied his orders, was what Brian was saying. I'd gotten my moment of glory, and now we were all going to pay.

Still, I didn't know if I wanted to hear anything stranger than what I'd been hearing almost daily since Pleasant Valley. But Avery wasn't really asking if we wanted to hear it. He was going to tell us, whether we liked it or not. For a second I looked at the TV screen. It was a "Great Moments" about the Second World War. Some planes were bombing a ship. Pearl Harbor. Billows of smoke rose toward the sky.

"Listen, dudes," said Avery. "Remember that

redheaded kid from Pleasant Valley, the guy you were guarding last night, Tom?"

Of course I did. In fact I was having an unpleasantly clear vision of the last time I saw that kid, waiting for me, hanging around after the game.

"Well, he was waiting near the locker room last night when I got through changing."

"I saw him there, too," I told Avery. "I thought he was some kind of pervert or groupie or something. Cruising. He gave me the creeps."

"That's what I thought," Avery said. "And I was sure that was the story. Because listen to this. When I walked past him, he pressed a scrap of paper with his phone number on it into my hand."

"The guy was asking Avery for a date!" Brian said. "Can you believe that, one of the Pleasant Valley losers was asking Avery for a date!"

It made me doubly glad that I hadn't stopped and talked to him. That was way more than I wanted to deal with last night. Besides, I might have missed running into Becca. I thought about him fouling me. And about his face when I lay there. How he was mouthing the words, "I'm sorry." I couldn't keep from shuddering.

"That's what I figured," Avery said. "That the guy was totally gay. Plus I was tired, and the game had been so bizarre. Man, I was *not* in the mood. I said, 'Excuse me, dude, what *is* this? Are you, like, asking me out?'

" 'Believe me, this isn't like that,' said the red-haired guy. 'Trust me. It's a matter of life and death. Call me in an hour.'

"Life and death sounded pretty heavy," Avery went on. "You don't hear *that* every day. Plus by now I had the definite feeling that this wasn't about dating. So I got home and called the guy."

"What did he say?" I asked.

"Well, it was strange. He talked very fast, like someone was about to come into the room, or listening in, or something. I mean, he was so nervous that he got me nervous, too. He was so freaking paranoid that he made poor Silas sound like the Buddha.

"He told me that dozens of kids have disappeared from Pleasant Valley. Starting right after the shootings. They got this new grief and crisis counselor, like we did, and a few days later, students started leaving school. Everybody was saying they were taking a few days off because they were so stressed out and depressed and in crisis about the murders. But then they didn't come back again. They *still* haven't come back. And kids have started saying that their e-mails are being read, and they're being asked to tell on one another."

"Just like here," Brian said.

"Just like Silas warned us," said Avery. "The editor of their high-school newspaper was one of the first ones sent away because he published something about the disappearances."

"Then they're doing better than us," said Brian. "We never even *had* a newspaper."

"They've lost a lot more people," Avery said. "I mean, a *lot*. Only three kids from Central have been sent away, but a major chunk of the Pleasant

Valley student body is permanently missing. It's as if they got a head start because the shootings happened there. Like they're in the accelerated program—but we're headed in the same direction. The redheaded guy said that someone at Pleasant Valley found out that there are detention camps for teens spread out all over the country. Masquerading as rehab centers and wilderness programs. Operation Turnaround is a nationwide deal. And those who don't cooperate are getting killed. Taken out and shot. And then they claim that they were trying to escape."

"Like Stephanie," said Brian.

"Duh," Avery said.

"Come on," I said. "It's a pretty unlikely story, don't you think? Did you believe the guy?" The truth was, *I* believed the guy. It no longer seemed unlikely at all. But still, I wanted to hear Brian and Avery deny it. I wanted them to convince me that it wasn't true.

"I believed him," said Avery. "And it started to

make sense. I mean, whatever made us think that this was all Dr. Willner's idea? The orders, the rules, the whole concept—it had to be coming from somewhere else. Whatever made us imagine that Willner was smart enough to think all this up on his own? *Of course* it's happening other places, it's way bigger than just some little *problem* we're having here at Central—"

"Oh, man," said Brian. "This is so intense. I need a second to think."

"That's about all the time we've got," Avery said. "About a second. Because the kid from Pleasant Valley said the whole process just begins going faster and faster. Once it starts, it accelerates. Practically the only ones left in his school are the ones on the teams and the extracurricular groups, the chorus, the orchestra, the kids that they can keep sending out into the world to make people believe that things are still all right, they're normal, that they're even—ugh, I hate this word, *healing*—at Pleasant Valley. But the truth is that the school is practically emptied out. There's hardly anyone there. It's down to maybe fifty students in the entire school. They're planning to send the last ones away to these camps pretty soon, and then they're just going to close the whole place down. There's this rumor that they're planning to round them all up at once, on some perfectly normal school day when no one's expecting it."

Well, great. Here we were, apparently at the heart of a national conspiracy, and Dr. Willner—the head of our own local commando unit—was especially mad at me. And over what? A basketball game? The fact that it seemed to make so much sense, and that it was so much worse than I'd thought, made me even more jumpy than I was already.

For a moment we all felt sort of drained. We sat there and watched Bus TV. On the screen, the A-bomb mushroom cloud was rising lazily over Japan.

—"Plus the guy was saying all kinds of other

things," Avery murmured, almost to himself. "Like that most of the information we get on Bus TV is total crap. That most of these Moments in History are completely fake. Like now. Look at that."

We all fell silent and listened. On TV, the announcer was saying that the A-bombs which ended the war were dropped on two wilderness areas, Hiroshima and Nagasaki.

"Dude," said Avery. "Listen to that. I don't think that's true."

"How stupid *were* we?" said Brian.

"We weren't watching," I said. "We weren't paying attention."

Now we stared up at the TV, and I had the strangest feeling. Namely, that it was watching *us*. It was almost as if I saw something, a camera lens, glinting behind the surface, the way I used to see this funny glint from the artificial lens in my grandma's eyes after she got her cataract operation.

I guess we all had the same thought at once.

Brian said, "Smile, you're on Candid Camera."

Avery whispered, "Da-*amn*."

• • •

That morning, as soon as I got through the metal detectors, the first kids who saw me started cheering. Someone slapped me on the back. At first I was confused, thinking that somehow everyone knew I'd stood up to Dr. Willner. But of course, that wasn't it. It was just that I'd won last night's game. And maybe everyone had had the same guilty desire—they'd *really* wanted to beat Pleasant Valley, to get even with the place where all our trouble had started.

It all seemed so ironic that I was finally someone important, somebody people called out to and greeted by name as I walked down the hall. And I wasn't even going to get a chance to enjoy it before I got sent away. Though maybe . . . the thought crossed my mind that maybe all the attention might protect me for a few days. Maybe Dr. Willner might wait awhile before he did something drastic to someone who, at least for the moment, the whole school considered some kind of hero. And then, soon enough, everyone would forget about me, and Dr. Willner could do what he wanted.

All during homeroom I waited to be called to the front office. But nothing happened, there was no call, no one delivered the note with my name on it.

In assembly Dr. Willner talked about last night's game. He never mentioned our team, which was fairly strange to begin with—the fact that a school official would only praise our opponents. He talked about how inspiring it was that Pleasant Valley had played so well. He said it was a model of healing and recovery, and that we should try to follow their inspirational example.

For the millionth time I had that feeling that Dr. Willner knew everything. He knew that the Pleasant Valley kid had told Avery, and that the three of us knew what was going on. He was telling us in secret code, in the middle of assembly, that the same things that were happening at Pleasant Valley were going to start happening to us. And soon.

Walking into my first-period class, I practically had my eyes closed, that's how sure I was that I was about to get the note ordering me to come see Dr. Willner—by last period, at the latest.

"Are you sure there's nothing for me?" I asked Mrs. Davis.

There wasn't. There was nothing. But that didn't necessarily mean anything. Willner could be playing with me, like a cat with a mouse. Tomorrow I could come in and find out that they'd already enrolled me in Operation Turnaround.

Needless to say, I was on edge, and I pretty much stayed there. And so when someone knocked on the door in the middle of social studies class, I was positive that my time had come. I braced myself and prayed: Please don't let this be what I think. I thought about Mrs. Ridley. And Stephanie. And Silas, wherever he was.

Bug Boy hovered in the doorway. He stared straight at me. I almost stood up.

But then he said Avery's name. And I wondered if that was why I'd been spared—if Dr. Willner had been so busy thinking about Avery that he'd forgotten about me for the present.

Avery got up. He looked at me and Brian. He said, "Dudes, if I don't come back, make sure my mom and dad know I was last seen heading for Dr. Willner's office."

But Avery showed up for lunch. He was sitting in the cafeteria by the time Brian and I arrived. He'd gotten himself a huge plate, a triple helping of French fries, like he always did whenever they served those soggy, frozen crinkle fries. But that day he didn't eat any of them. He just kept squirting them with ketchup.

I said, "What's this new thing with ketchup, dude?" But Avery didn't smile.

"It was bad," he told Brian and me. "Dude, they had me on *film*. On the bus this morning. Plus they'd already *edited* it. How did they get this together so fast? This is totally gruesome."

On the one hand, it was horrifying that they'd been filming us all the time. On the other hand, I was—well, I was *relieved*. Because when they first called Avery in, I'd had the most terrible thought. I wondered if maybe someone had told on him, reported what he'd been saying, the way someone had reported Mrs. Ridley for protecting Becca for having her cell phone. And I'd known that the only person who could have told on Avery was Brian. The fact was, I'd rather have known they were filming us and reading our e-mail and tapping our phones than find out that one of my best friends was ratting out the other. I looked at Brian, and I wanted to hug him, that's how guilty I felt about having suspected him, even for a minute.

"My mom and my dad were already there," Avery was saying. "In Dr. Willner's office. He showed them the tape on his computer monitor. They'd shot it on digital, right? Plus, it was perfect audio quality. How the hell did they manage that?

"And there I am in living color saying all this stuff about detention camps for kids, how it's spreading all over the country. They've edited out the part about my hearing this from the Pleasant Valley kid. So it's like I've made it up myself, like *I'm* on drugs, like I've dreamed it all up. *I* thought I was a freaking lunatic. That's how insane I sounded. If it had been up to me, I would have had myself committed on the spot.

"Of course my mom and dad are completely shocked. They're watching with their mouths open. I sound way much further out than Silas at his paranoid worst. They're wondering if I'm high or something. And Dr. Willner has swung right into full grief-and-crisis-psychology-counselor mode. He's droning on and on about how I am exhibiting symptoms of paranoia, common symptoms of drug use, or at least of extreme stress, symptoms that are often predicative of *extreme* behavioral problems and even violence.

"My mom and dad are looking at me as if

they've never seen me before. They're wondering; How long has this been going on? How could they have missed it?

"So Dr. Willner says, 'There are marvelous facilities to deal with this. Programs that only last a week or two at most and get extraordinary results.'" He's telling my parents that the state has these fabulous intervention programs, these weeklong intensive residency camps for 'kids at risk.' Like *me*.

"Meanwhile my mom's asking if this couldn't be treated somehow without my leaving home. Dude, it turns out I'm in *treatment* already. They're just discussing *how*. Hammering out the details.

"And Willner says, 'Look at it this way. These places are very pleasant. And free. Think of it as a weeklong retreat—like summer camp—all at the state's expense. All expenses paid. Lots of parents shell out fortunes for programs just like that.'

"He made it sound as if I'd been *chosen* for some kind of special honor. That's how lucky Willner made my parents feel. And it was like they'd been brainwashed. I didn't recognize them. I didn't know who they'd turned into, letting some white man convince them that their kid needed to be sent away."

Brian and I let that "white man" pass, as if we hadn't heard it.

Then I said, "Avery, man, have your parents been reading the e-mails from school?"

"I guess," said Avery. "I'm pretty sure they have."

"What about it?" Brian said. "My mom does. All the parents read them."

I couldn't believe I'd figured it out about the e-mails, and that Brian and Avery hadn't. Then I remembered: It wasn't me. It was Becca who'd put it together. I reminded myself to tell Brian how important it was to get his mom to stop reading them. But that was a whole other subject; there wasn't time for that now. Avery's parents were already lost, there was nothing I could do about it.

And at the present moment we had to concentrate on helping Avery.

I said, "Avery, man, you're not actually *going*? Are you?"

"Tomorrow." Avery shrugged.

"You're not," said Brian. "Don't. Run away. I'd leave right now. Sneak out. Go home and get some money and clothes. Go to Boston or something. Just lay low, keep a low profile till everything blows over."

"Call us," I said. "We'll figure out how to get you more money."

"They can trace his cell phone," said Brian.

"Then call us from pay phones," I said.

Avery wasn't going for the fantasy. "I'm not running away," he said. "Who can say that things will be any better in Boston? It's practically the dead of winter. Plus they're probably rounding up the runaways first. They've been doing that for years—long before Pleasant Valley. And maybe they're telling the truth about wherever they're sending me to. Maybe the place *is* okay. Maybe it's just for a week. Maybe when I come back after that, I'll be smart enough not to shoot my mouth off right in front of the cameras on the bus."

"Dude, what *happened* to you in Willner's office?" I said. "Did they medicate you already? I mean, what are you *on*?"

"I don't think anything," Avery said. "Unless it was in the air. Let's just wait and see what happens, okay? I'll see you guys in a week or two. And listen? If I were you guys, I'd shut up when you're on the bus. And I'd at least pretend to be watching Bus TV. Because, dude"—he looked at me—"I saw you on the videotape, zoning out, not paying attention to the program, staring out the window. And don't think Willner didn't notice."

It just didn't make sense that Avery would have caved in so quickly. But maybe it had something to do with the fact that his parents were so ready to let him go, that they didn't stick by him, that he felt as if they'd been brainwashed. Maybe they'd talked him into going, or maybe their being so quick to get with Dr. Willner's program had sapped his will to resist. He'd always been close to his mom and dad, so it must have come as a huge shock.

The next day, some kids who lived near Avery said they saw a police car come for him, and at the last moment he'd started to struggle, and his parents had stood in the doorway, smiling and waving. Like robots.

Avery didn't come back to school, though we waited and waited.

We were fine with it the first week, and the second. But after that, Brian and I got that same heavy feeling we'd gotten when Silas left.

Obviously this was much worse, since now two kids were gone, and they were both our best friends. It seemed a lot more than twice as bad, though I couldn't exactly say why. For one thing, I felt guilty. Naturally, the thought crossed my mind that Avery had taken a bullet for me. Avery had saved me. Because as it turned out, whatever happened with Avery that morning on the bus had distracted Willner and made him forget about the game the night before. At least for the moment.

I never heard another word about the Pleasant Valley game from Dr. Willner. It was as if it hadn't happened. And Brian and I didn't discuss it. We were too scared. We knew that the bullet we'd just dodged was still out there, flying around with our names on it. And that seemed like part of the program, too. Sometimes you broke the rules and suffered the consequences. And sometimes, like Becca said, you didn't. It was all meant to throw you off balance, to make you realize that they could do anything, make and break any rules they wanted.

It was depressing, sitting alone with Brian at lunch and on the bus. And so when Becca started sitting with us, Brian was nice to her, even though she was nothing like the hot girls he went out with. Becca always sat next to me now. I guess that meant she was my girlfriend. Becca and I never talked about that. We kissed when no one was looking. I liked her a lot.

We talked on the phone, but cautiously. We were careful about what we said. And I couldn't help thinking how different it would have been if all of this had happened before the shootings at Pleasant Valley. Maybe we would have said different things on the phone if we hadn't always been afraid that someone was listening. But then again, I didn't know what those different things would have been.

As it turned out, I began to think that the reason I never got into trouble about the basketball game was because Dr. Willner had other things on his mind.

He had other problems to deal with.

For example, the graffiti.

twelve

ONE MORNING WE ARRIVED at school just in time to find Miss Prune and Bug Boy frantically trying to clean off something someone had written in bright orange paint, in shaky letters, on the main front door.

Brian and I grabbed each other.

The graffiti said WHERE IS SILAS?

"It wasn't you, was it?" Brian said. "You didn't write that, did you?"

"Are you kidding?" I said. I was flattered that Brian might even *think* it was me.

We knew assembly was going to be rough. But somehow we hadn't imagined that things had gotten to the point at which Dr. Willner could totally drop the mask of the caring, sympathetic, psychologically minded grief and crisis counselor and let us see his true self—how enraged and deranged he really was.

He had the PA volume turned up as high as it would go, and there was lots of static and feedback, so that it was physically painful to listen to him as he launched into his tirade. His face was nearly purple as he stood alone on stage and thundered and screamed.

"Infractions such as this morning's graffiti incident are completely unacceptable and will not be tolerated. Defacing school property is bad enough—vandalizing the very things your parents have worked so hard to provide you with, destroying the things our government guarantees, our basic freedoms . . . I can not believe that a Central High student would do such a thing. And what is even worse is for someone to exploit, to exploit—for obscure and stupid and selfish reasons, something no doubt connected with *adolescent rebellion*—to exploit the name of an unfortunate Central student whose problems mandated—*mandated*—that he get help. Everyone knows where the young man is—in a residential treatment facility! So what exactly is the point, what statement is being made by the author of that graffiti that is such a hideous stain on the face and good name and the whole reputation of the school?"

Dr. Willner ranted on for so long that we began to realize that he was cutting into the next period and they'd suspended the bells. It lasted for so long that—as loud and frightening as it was—after a while it lulled us.

I was thinking of something Brian had said that morning, something about his mom. He'd tried to tell her what was happening at school, and she'd sort of lost interest, she wasn't really listening, she just mumbled monosyllables. It was like *he* used to sound when she asked him about school. Sure, good, fine, everything's fine. Can I go to my room now? It worried me when Brian said that, because I'd thought of Brian's mom as an ally, as a major reinforcement we could call in when it got to that point. And now if she wasn't there for us, it made me feel more alone. If only my mom were still around, she would have talked to Brian's mom and to the other parents. She would have known exactly what was happening and what had to be done

Brian said, "I think you're right, man. I think it *is* the school e-mail. And it's so brilliant of them. I mean, why bother sending a race of alien pod people to take over the planet when you've got the Internet? It certainly puts a whole new spin on the idea of a computer virus. All you have to do is open a message and it infects your *brain*." And then it was as if he'd remembered he was talking about his *mom*. He'd said, "I don't know what to do. I really don't. I don't know how to make her stop reading it. And mostly I don't know if it's already too late."

Now I could tell from the shifting in the seats around me that Dr. Willner had just said something that was totally rocking the house.

"What did he say?" I asked Becca.

"Hush. Listen," Becca said.

"Check this out," said Brian.

"The perpetrator will be caught. He or she *will* be caught. And we are prepared to do anything required to make sure that this happens. In this auditorium right now there are at least two people. At least one of you did it. And at least one of you knows who did it. Which makes that second person an accomplice. And that person will be brought to justice."

Instinctively we looked around. What were we thinking we'd see? I felt like I was the one who did it, even though I hadn't. At the same time, I was afraid that everyone would think it was me. After all, Silas was my friend. And since the Pleasant Valley game, I was a lot more visible than I'd been before.

Was it Brian? I didn't think so. Though I wouldn't have been completely surprised.

"So we are going to take extreme measures to make sure that one of these two—or more—culprits comes forward and makes a full confession. Or that someone tells us who *should* be making a full confession. If my office does not receive this information by three o'clock this afternoon, a curfew will be imposed on all Central High students. A ten o'clock curfew will go into effect, on weekdays and weekends alike, and the local police and state troopers will be instructed to enforce it."

Ten o'clock? On weekends? Everybody groaned.

"Parents have been advised to monitor their nightly e-mails even more closely than before," Dr. Willner said. "And students are even more strongly advised to check with their parents. Especially if they leave school today before we announce the final decisions about the probable consequences of these serious offenses. Students should also know that we have conferred with the town council, and we have been empowered to pass this curfew as a law. Which is why the state troopers and police will naturally be involved. . . ."

That was all anyone talked about all day. Classes were basically over. The teachers tried to keep some semblance of order, but it was hopeless. Everyone was whispering and passing notes. It was total chaos.

And the funny thing was, in the past, at least one of the teachers would have flipped out and sent at least several students down to the office. But now none of the teachers did. Even the teachers who seemed most changed still hadn't lost it completely, so maybe the e-mails the teachers were getting weren't working as well—not yet— as the ones they sent the parents. The teachers knew what was at stake for all of them, and for us. No one had forgotten Mrs. Ridley. And so the teachers thought a million times before they sent us to Dr. Willner. Because by now, of course, everyone knew, or at least suspected: A trip to Dr. Willner's office might mean a little threatening conversation. Or it might mean a one-way ticket to Operation Turnaround.

So you might say that the discipline loosened at school at the same time as it tightened. Or maybe it just loosened in class. Anyway, we learned less. Pop quizzes were a thing of the past, and we somehow knew that no one would fail a course ever again. We hardly had any homework.

And no one ever talked about college.

It was hard to be focused or energetic. The only energy, really, was fear. And you tried not to feel it. In the evenings, when I got home, I watched MTV and played video games.

Every so often I watched the evening news to see if they reported that students were disappearing from high schools all over the country. After all, they used to run stories when kids died at those wilderness rehab camps. That was how we first heard about places like Operation Turnaround. But now the news never mentioned it. Did that prove that Silas and Avery were right—that there was some nationwide conspiracy, and that now the media was involved?

One evening at dinner Dad said, "I hear there's a ten o'clock curfew."

"Where did you hear that?" I asked, hardly breathing.

"On the radio," he said.

I thought, Excellent! So my dad still wasn't reading the e-mails.

"How outrageous is *that*?" I said.

"I don't know," said my dad. "In theory, I'm against it. Kids have their constitutional rights. Etcetera. But the truth is, Tomster—"

"Don't call me that," I said.

"All right, Tom. The question is, do I *mind* your being home every night by ten? No, in fact I do not. The roads are full of drunken maniacs. I hate what goes on at the mall. And am I going to fight against your being home by ten? I don't think so."

"What if I get arrested for being out late?" I said.

"Then we'll deal with that then," said my dad.

"They're *not* doing this for my own good," I said. "For our health and safety. It's a punishment thing. Dr. Willner's in a rage because some kid wrote 'Where is Silas?' on the front door of the school, and no one knows who did it."

"I hate graffiti," said my dad. "It makes everything ugly. You should have seen Boston in the seventies, before your mom and I moved out here. Anyway, I ran into Silas's mom the other day at the market."

I asked, "Did she say how Silas is doing?" Brian and I had stopped calling, we'd gotten so tired of hearing her say that Silas was doing great. What if Silas had been killed? Would she have known? Would she have told us?

Dad said, "She told me that Silas was doing great, that he'd be home soon. Apparently his drug problem was a little more serious than anyone thought."

"Wrong. It wasn't," I said. "I know how bad it was." But I stopped myself right there. Drugs were not the point.

I said, "Did she seem . . . strange to you?"

"Strange how?" asked my dad.

"I don't know. Sort of robotic."

"She did seem a little spacey," said Dad. "But

then she always was. Actually . . . the truly strange thing was she asked me if I was reading all my e-mails from school. Why do you think she would have cared, considering Silas isn't at school anymore? I mean, what was it to *her*?"

"What did you tell her?" I said.

"I told her of course I am. Jeez, I didn't want to seem like Mr. Negligent Parent."

"And *are* you?" I couldn't help asking, though I was pretty certain he wasn't.

"Are you kidding?" said my dad. "Who's got time? Life is short."

We both got very quiet. Then I said, "What if I get sent away? Like Avery and Silas?"

My dad thought a moment. He said, "No one's going to send you away. Just don't do anything stupid."

Things settled down for a couple of days. Then one morning we got to school, and the guards were scrubbing off letters. This time it was in purple, across a bank of lockers—in dripping blood purple, actually.

The letters said WHERE IS AVERY?

We all marched into assembly. This time Dr. Willner started slow, talking about the forensic graphologists who had been called in to determine that so far all the graffiti had been done by the same student. Probably a lone male. With antisocial tendencies.

We could have told him that the same person did both, without the forensic graphologist. First of all, it was the same writing. And second of all, this was not some copycat thing, like phoning in a bomb scare. There were no bomb scares anymore. And I almost missed them.

"For this reason," Dr. Willner shouted, "it is even more important to identify the possibly dangerous, possibly violent personality behind this egregious crime."

It wasn't me. It wasn't me. Did Dr. Willner know that?

"Until the culprit is caught, we—again working in cooperation with the town authorities—have decided that Central High students will be prohibited from going to the mall. At any hour. It is bad enough to have a possibly violent sociopath in our midst. But how can we subject the general populace to that risk by setting this potential killer loose in a place filled with innocent shoppers, men and women and babies? Of course, as soon as we find out who is responsible for these graffiti incidents, mall privileges will be immediately restored."

The amazing thing was that, even after this, none of the kids turned anyone in. I'll bet some of them were tempted to report someone they didn't like just so we could all go to the mall again. But I guess it proved how honest we are—that basic kid sense of justice. We hated not being able to go to the mall, but we weren't going to sacrifice some innocent kid who hadn't done anything wrong. No one seemed to know who *had* done it, which saved us all the problem of figuring out what we would have done if we caught someone in the act of painting tomorrow's big question.

Anyway, I expected the worst. I walked around in constant dread of being called into Dr. Willner's office and accused. I was an obvious suspect. Silas and Avery were my best friends.

The next question—painted in red this time, this time on the cafeteria wall—was: WHERE IS STEPHANIE?

A couple of kids saw it. Word got around. At assembly Dr. Willner announced that lunch in the cafeteria was canceled indefinitely. Students were supposed to go to their homerooms and eat their sandwiches at their desks. Students who expected to buy lunch were advised to share with students who had brought theirs, and to think about the consequences, and about what it would be like if lunchroom was canceled forever. Which was only one of the punishments that were now under consideration in the event that the graffiti writer did not come forward and identify himself.

No lunch? Well, we could live with that. It was as if Stephanie's name worked a kind of magic on us. Now even if we had known who was doing it, I don't think we would have told. No matter how they threatened us, no matter what they did.

Because for most of us, the memory of Stephanie was a lot more powerful than that of Avery and Silas. And even though the guys were my best friends, I understood that Stephanie was different. Maybe because she was a girl, or because she was so pretty and everybody loved her. Maybe because of her tragic life, the dying brother she nursed, the red ribbon. Maybe because she went first, right at the beginning, when she was still so pure, before the rest of us got the chance to be afraid, and so we hadn't protested or said anything, and we had made our little compromises. Maybe because she'd done nothing wrong except to have worn a red ribbon. And of course there was no maybe about the fact that she was dead.

Somehow it kicked everything up to a whole other level. It took things further than just our friends, two kids from the Smart Jocks. And it was almost as if Dr. Willner were aware of it, too, as if he knew that things were escalating. Some tiny pocket of resistance was smoldering under the surface. More and more often in morning assembly, Dr. Willner insulted us.

One morning he spoke for almost two hours. He told us that we had no ambition, no integrity, no courage, no intelligence, no common sense, no honesty—not like kids used to have. We were stupid, we were hopeless. . . .

Were the spy cameras rolling? What if an outsider saw this? The teachers had their heads down. The auditorium was silent. Becca sat between me and Brian, and at some point she took both our hands, and she just held them. It made me think of the memorial services they'd held in Pleasant Valley and shown on TV, right after the shootings. Eveyone had been holding hands, sitting there with their heads bowed, some of the kids were crying. . . .

Dr. Willner ended the assembly by saying— well, shouting—that if the culprit was not found and dealt with in a timely fashion, our punishment would be so terrible that they (and he didn't say who *they* were) were still debating the limits of the terrible consequences we would suffer.

thirteen

T HAT AFTERNOON I WALKED BECCA home from school. It was a habit we'd fallen into. I hated the bus now, anyway. I couldn't even pretend to watch Bus TV, and I couldn't talk to Brian, knowing the cameras were watching. I'd go with Becca to her house, and her mom would drive me home later. Sometimes they'd have an early dinner, and I'd stay, and her dad would drive me back. Her dad was quiet, like her mom. And also friendly and nice. He seemed to like me, or at least not to have any strong feelings one way or the other about my being there.

Usually when Becca and I got to her house, we'd go straight into the kitchen and sit at the counter drinking soda and eating chips and talking. Sometimes we'd make out on the walk to her house, but we always stopped before we got there.

On the day when someone wrote WHERE IS STEPHANIE?—a school day we finished without ever hearing what terrible consequences Dr. Willner had in mind—we got to her house, and Becca said, "Let's go in through the garage door."

"Why?" I said. "It's out of the way."

"I don't know," she said. "No reason. Let's do something different."

As soon as Becca pushed the button that made the garage door fold up, my eye tracked to the far corner, on the floor. There were three open buckets of house paint, and another one that was still closed. Plus a large brush for each bucket, with the paint still on it.

The colors were unmistakable. The orange of WHERE IS SILAS? The purple of WHERE IS AVERY? The red of WHERE IS STEPHANIE?

I understood what it meant right away. But I didn't want to admit it. I thought, Well, so what? What did that mean? It was paint, that was all. Circumstantial evidence. It didn't mean Becca had done it. But I knew. Becca had painted the graffiti. And she wanted me to know it.

For about a million reasons, I wished she hadn't told me. I wasn't sure how I felt about my girlfriend doing something that I would never have had the courage to do in a million years. For another thing, I didn't need to know. Because it made *me* that second person Dr. Willner was looking for—the accomplice. I had a brief fantasy about being picked up and tortured until I was forced to reveal that Becca had done it. I would die, I would go to my grave with the secret still locked inside me.

But why did Becca have to let me know? Did she want me to respect and admire her more? Was she trying to find out if I really liked her? If I cared about her enough to keep a secret like that? Or maybe she just couldn't stand it anymore, being the only one who knew.

"They're looking for a male," Becca said. "A loner male. With antisocial tendencies. They've got a little profiling problem."

"Brilliant," I said. "Are you totally crazy? Are you completely out of your mind?"

Becca's face was shining, she was so happy that I finally knew. I was flattered that she trusted me so much. But I still wished I hadn't found out.

"What's that for?" I pointed to the unopened can of paint.

"One last question," said Becca.

"Absolutely not," I said. "Give it up. Right now."

"You can't stop me," Becca said.

"I wish I could," I said. But to tell the truth, I didn't know if that was true. I wouldn't have stopped her. I didn't want to. What I really meant was, I hoped they didn't catch her.

Weirdly, we started kissing right then. I guess it's embarrassing to admit, but it was sort of a turn-on. The danger, and the bravery, and the sudden awareness that if Becca got caught, she would be in more trouble than anyone at Central had ever gotten into. Ever. And now I was an accomplice. We kissed, standing there in the garage, right in the midst of the smelly paint rags and garden equipment and the auto exhaust fumes.

And of course that had a big influence on what happened next.

I wish I could say that my decision came at a quiet moment of reflection and common sense, of bravery and resolve. I wish I could say that I'd thought it over and decided if Becca was in this, I was, too. I was in it, together with her. But the truth is that I decided—or didn't decide—at the moment we were kissing. By the time we'd come up for air, somehow it was all arranged.

I was going with her. I wouldn't actually do the painting, but I would be her lookout when she wrote that one last question.

"It's a two-part question," Becca said. "Where is Jerry Gargiulo? And where is Mrs. Ridley?"

"What about Mr. Trent?"

"Let's save him for the next round. Believe me,

plenty more kids and teachers are going to be disappearing."

"You and I will be the next round," I said.
"Where is Becca? Where is Tom?"

"In that case," said Becca, "someone else will
have to paint it."

The plan was to go back to school at nine in
the evening. It was the school downtime. There
was hardly anyone there, maybe a few stray people
left over from some parents' meeting. And there
had been fewer and fewer parents' meetings lately.
Or *any* kind of meetings—at least that we knew
about.

By nine, the night watchman wouldn't have
come in yet. And the evening janitor was just
going off his shift. But first he would go outside
for a smoke, as he did every evening, to the
bleachers by the tennis courts. And he'd leave the
side door open. And that was how we could sneak
in.

Everything happened exactly the way Becca said it would. I don't know how she'd figured it all out. I was extremely impressed.

On the way I offered to carry the paint for her, but she said she didn't want me to. In case we got caught.

I said, "You promised we weren't going to *get* caught."

"I haven't so far," she said.

Because it was a two-part question and because there were so many words, Becca had decided that the only wall big enough was the one down the length of the gym. I didn't want to go to the gym. After the game with Pleasant Valley, it had felt sort of cursed to me, sort of haunted and spooky. But this was Becca's project, her idea. I was just there as a lookout.

The school was empty and quiet. I loved it. I loved it the way you might love an obnoxious little kid when it finally fell asleep. The gym was dark. Becca gave me her flashlight. I stood near the door to the locker room and held the flashlight so she could see.

Becca began painting. I watched her arm move in long, steady swoops. WHERE . . . IS . . . JERRY . . . GARGIULO?

She was painting pretty quickly, but still it seemed to take forever. I was practically jumping out of my skin.

I whispered, "Isn't one question enough?"

And then I saw the second light.

It was another flashlight, another beam besides mine. At first it was confusing. I thought I'd somehow lost control of my light, and it was tracking over the gym.

But how could that have happened? I was holding mine steady so Becca could paint. Then someone threw on all the gym lights, and as my eyes got accustomed to the blazing brightness, I recognized Dr. Willner.

What was he doing here? How had he found us? How did he know? But of course it was perfect.

Who else would it have been? Who else would have cared enough? Who else would have been creeping around with a flashlight, in school, at nine o'clock in the evening? He knew someone was painting the messages at night. He'd promised to do whatever it took. Dr. Willner's face was monstrous, contorted with rage and hate. If he could have shot us both on the spot, and gotten away with it, I was sure he would have done it.

Becca and I screamed in unison. And then we froze like deer in the headlights. I mean, we *were* in the headlights. There was a moment of absolute quiet. Then Becca dropped her paintbrush and came over and grabbed my hand.

And we ran.

Why didn't they arrest us that night? That's what I expected to happen. Becca and I said good-bye as if we'd never see each other again. Becca was crying. She kept saying, "I'm sorry. I'm sorry. I'm so sorry I got you into this mess." And I kept saying,

"That's okay, it wasn't your fault. I did it to myself."

I didn't know if I believed that. But there wasn't time to figure out what I believed, or didn't.

Becca's mom drove me home. She didn't know what had happened. She probably thought the paint in the garage was for some kind of science project. If she'd read the e-mails, she would have realized. Which was another reason to be glad she hadn't read them.

All the way back to my house, I almost wished I could start crying and have Becca's mom ask me what was wrong, and then I could tell her the truth. I imagined burying my face in her shoulder and telling her that Becca had been busted by Dr. Willner for painting the graffiti, and I'd been caught along with her. And that we were both as good as dead—or anyway, as good as sent away to Operation Turnaround.

But it was Becca's decision, whether or not to tell her mom. I never would have told. If you didn't tell the school on someone, you certainly didn't tell their parents. And you didn't tell *anyone* when it was your girlfriend.

I didn't sleep at all that night. I kept listening for the sound of a cop car pulling up, for the screech of tires on gravel. Maybe I slept for an hour or two. I remember lying awake, deciding how I was going to tell my dad. Because I knew that this was my last chance, and that I had to be very clear. Because if I didn't convince them, there would be no one there to stand up for me when the cops came and got me like they'd come and gotten Avery. And the funny thing was, even though I was pretty sure my dad hadn't been brainwashed like the other parents, some nagging little voice in my head kept saying, What if he *had* been? What if he lets them come and get me?

I decided I would tell Dad and Clara together. I figured it might double my chances of someone taking me seriously. Also I decided to tell them early in the day. I don't know why, but I felt as if my story would seem more reasonable, more logical if

I told it in the morning. In broad daylight.

Not having slept, I was up long before my dad and Clara, which must have come as a shock. Usually on weekends I slept till one in the afternoon. That is, unless I was planning to hook up with my friends at the mall. But that didn't happen anymore. And anyway, there was just Brian. And we weren't allowed to go to the mall.

I decided to make coffee for Clara and my dad. So I was fussing around the kitchen when my dad came downstairs.

He jumped when he saw me.

"Tomster," he said.

I didn't say, "Don't call me that." Which was the second shock of the day. He felt he had to say something.

"I know you don't like me to call you that," he said. "I know it's what your mom called you. But sometimes I just forget and do it anyway. Or maybe part of me keeps doing it because I'm trying to hear her voice."

"That's okay," I said. "I know all that. Don't worry about it. It's not a problem."

"Are you feeling all right? You're up awfully early for a Saturday morning."

"I'm fine," I said. "I mean, sort of. I think we need to talk. Listen, I've got an idea. Why don't you and Clara and I go out to breakfast at the diner?"

My dad flinched at that: *We need to talk.* No one likes to hear that. But I think it was the first time that I ever actually suggested that my dad and Clara and I do anything together. And it made him so happy that he would have agreed no matter what he thought was coming. Who knows what he imagined? Maybe something about Becca and me. "Dad, I've got bad news for you. I've gotten my girlfriend pregnant."

If only that were what it was! I was suddenly filled with envy for all those kids who'd lived in the old days before Pleasant Valley, and who'd had to deal with whatever ordinary problem they'd had—and who'd thought that was serious trouble.

Considering what was ahead of us, we were all in a weirdly good mood as we piled into my dad's car and headed for the diner. I took it as a good sign that Nell, our favorite waitress, was working that day, since she usually worked the dinner shift, and hardly ever on weekends.

No one had to look at the menu. My dad and I ordered the breakfast special: two eggs over, bacon, home fries, toast. Clara ordered oatmeal.

"Live a little," my dad said.

"I'm trying to," said Clara.

I figured it was best if they heard what I had to say on a full stomach, so I waited until we were done. At last my dad pushed his plate away and said, "So didn't you say back at the house that you had something you wanted to talk about?"

"I guess I did," I said. Breakfast tasted so amazingly good, and I was so full and satisfied that, for a second, I almost let the whole thing drop. And then I remembered Becca and the paint, and the look on Dr. Willner's face when he caught us in the gym. And I knew that I had no choice.

"Listen," I said. "I know I've been telling you all this stuff about school, little by little. But you need to listen to *all* of it at once, you need to hear the whole story. Because the stuff that's been happening at school is really, *really* bad. Not only have we been losing all our rights, but now kids have been disappearing—"

"So you've been saying," my dad said.

"But now it's gotten worse. Avery's gone, too."

"*Avery's* gone?" said Clara.

Once I would have resented that, her acting like she knew my friends—or even just their names. But now I liked it that she seemed genuinely concerned.

"Why was Avery sent away?" asked my dad. "I didn't think he did drugs."

"It had nothing to do with drugs," I said. "It

was because he found out all this information about the lies they were telling on Bus TV, and how they were watching us with cameras. And just before he left—I mean, just before he got sent away—he talked to this guy from Pleasant Valley who said that their school had been nearly emptied out and practically shut down."

"It happens," said my dad. "It's normal. School boards shut down schools and build new ones—"

"But not because they've sent away all the students," I said. "There are hardly any kids left in their town. That redheaded guy I was guarding at the basketball game said that it had all begun there. They'd gotten a grief and crisis counselor, just like we have. Plus they had a head start because that's where the kids got shot. And now everything that happened at Pleasant Valley is going to happen to us, and now there's this thing with Becca, she's the one who's been painting the graffiti, and Dr. Willner caught me with her and—"

"Tom," said my dad. "Slow down. Take it easy.

Take it from the top. Let's hear the entire story. One thing at a time."

So I told them the whole story, in order. Everything that had happened. From the day our cell phones first went off, after Pleasant Valley. How Dr. Willner got there, how all the new rules started. How Stephanie got sent away, and then Silas. How Dr. Willner told us to lose the basketball game, and how I couldn't do it.

I tried to speak very slowly and calmly, without a trace of excitement or panic. I tried to sound like Avery making one of his legal arguments rather than like Silas getting wild and paranoid. Though not *so* paranoid, as it had turned out. Silas was right on the money. If only we had listened to him. It made me sad and happy at the same time, how easily I could still hear my friends' voices in my head, even though both of them were gone.

When I finished, the silence lasted a long time. Until finally my dad said, "Tom, why didn't you tell me?"

"I tried to," I said. "I kept trying. Remember?" There was more that I wanted to say, but I didn't know how, or I couldn't. Like how I'd kept trying to convince myself that things were still normal, that it wasn't as bad as it seemed. And I certainly couldn't talk about those moments when I'd worried that he wouldn't take me seriously or that he'd let me get sent away, or allow himself to get brainwashed, like the other parents.

"This is horrible," Clara said. "This is terrifying. We've got to do something, say something, tell someone—"

"Wait," I said. "It gets worse." And then I explained—as slowly and clearly as I could—about me and Becca and the paint.

"So I guess we're next," I said. "You should have seen Dr. Willner's face."

"Hold on. Calm down. No one's going to send you away," said my dad. "That would have to be over my dead body."

Clara knocked on the table, then looked

around. "There's no wood in this place to knock on," she said.

"We'll figure something out," said my dad. "You are definitely *not* going to be sent away to some detention camp."

Just hearing him say that was such a relief, I nearly burst out crying. I was so glad they believed me! I was also glad that I'd waited till after breakfast to tell them. Because I could see, from how drawn their faces had gotten—Clara was especially white—and from their shocked expressions that they wouldn't have been able to eat a bite after I got through.

"So what do we do now?" said Clara.

"I guess we should talk to the other parents," said my dad.

"That's not going to work," I said. "Avery's and Silas's mom and dad let them be sent away. And even Brian's mom has totally caved in. She's been saying that the school may be on the right track."

"*Brian's* mom said that?" said my dad. And the

way he said it made me wonder if maybe he hadn't had the tiniest bit of a crush on her.

"Yup," I said. "How strange is that?"

"Extremely strange," said my dad.

"I think it's the e-mails," I said. "I think they brainwashed the parents."

I expected my dad to say I was making that part up, letting my imagination run wild. But instead all he said was, "I *knew* there was a reason not to read that time-consuming crap."

Then Clara said, "I've got an idea. I just want to check something out." She rummaged around in her purse for a while, then said, "Darn, I forgot my phone. Can I borrow yours?"

My dad produced his cell phone, and I intercepted it as he handed it over to Clara. For just a minute, I wanted to grab it and call Becca and tell her that my dad and Clara believed me, that maybe things were looking up, maybe help was on the way. But then I thought that if Becca's phone was tapped, I didn't want anyone hearing me say that. For that matter, I didn't want them knowing where I was, or who I was with, or what we were planning. Not that we were planning anything yet. But we might be soon.

I gave Dad's phone to Clara. Who was she going to call?

Clara dialed information. She said, "Can I have the number of Pleasant Valley High School?"

"It's Saturday, remember?" I said. "No one's going to be there."

"Let's just see what happens," Clara said.

She dialed the number they gave her. Then she listened for a minute or so. When she put the phone down, she was even paler than she had been before.

"They said the number was disconnected."

"It's Saturday," my dad said.

"Disconnected," repeated Clara.

"Well, maybe they just changed it—"

Clara said, "Have we got plans for the day? Plans that can't be changed? Because I've suddenly got an idea. A little . . . field trip I want to take."

"Fine," I said. "I'm not doing much." I tried not to think how, not so very long ago, I might have been getting ready right about now to go meet Silas, Avery, and Brian at the mall.

"We're in your hands," Dad said.

"Can I drive?" said Clara.

"Sure," said my dad. "Are you going to tell us where we're going?"

"When we get there," Clara said.

fourteen

BUT AS IT TURNED OUT, we knew awhile before we got there—in fact, as soon as we turned off the highway at the Pleasant Valley exit. It felt so strange to see the sign. It was almost as if those two words, Pleasant Valley, had become some kind of dark private secret. So what were they doing there, written on a road sign, right out on the interstate, where everyone could see them?

It took a long time to find the school, especially considering how small a town Pleasant Valley is. We drove around and around the neat streets lined with well-kept houses. We passed some little kids riding their bikes, but no one my age. No one was shooting hoops in the driveways or washing cars or raking leaves for moms and dads. Not that it meant anything. After all, it wasn't noon yet. Most kids my age would be sleeping.

So maybe I was imagining that the houses looked sad. Most of the curtains were drawn tight, even the windows seemed dark and turned in on themselves. Maybe I was imagining that the houses looked like homes from which all the older kids had been sent away.

Most towns had signs telling you where the schools were, icons of caps and gowns—if only to help visiting sports teams figure out where the games were. But there were no signs here, though I spotted a few sawed-off posts that maybe used to have signs. They reminded me of the blank spot on the library shelves when I'd gone to try and find a book on Stalin.

"Maybe they leveled the building," said my dad. "Just wiped it off the map."

"I don't think so," said Clara. "I'm trying to remember how the school building looked on the news. Where it stood exactly in relation to the mountains."

For the first time I could see the point of Clara's

nature-girl thing. If we had to head into the woods and survive on nuts and wild berries, it might not be so terrible to have someone like Clara along.

The three of us fell silent. I guess we were all thinking of the TV footage of the state troopers and the emergency medical workers carrying the stretchers with the pulled-up blankets out of Pleasant Valley. It had only been six months or so, but it seemed like several lifetimes ago. Several of *my* lifetimes, for sure. So much had happened since.

Clara wasn't giving up. She took a winding road out of town, and there, a mile or so on the left, was Pleasant Valley High School. Clara pulled up the driveway and parked in front of the school.

Or anyway, what *used* to be the school. The place was a total wreck. How could a building have gone downhill so fast? It looked not only deserted, but as if it had been empty for years. They must have sent those last few kids away to Operation Turnaround right after the basketball game. That's what the redheaded guy had said they were going to do. He'd said they would round them all up at once. And maybe his telling us was the last straw, the final push, the reason they decided to go ahead and do it.

Scraps of yellow crime-scene tape flapped from the trees and the lampposts, relics of the shootings, ragged little souvenirs that—after all these months—no one had bothered to get rid of. It made the place look like one of those front yards that had gotten toilet-papered on Halloween.

"It looks like Pompeii," my dad said.

"Haunted," said Clara. "Spooky."

"Let's get out of here," I said. "Let's just go, okay?" It was not only sad but confusing. I knew it was Pleasant Valley, but I kept seeing *my* school— picturing how Central would look after we were all gone. It felt like those corny movies and plays, goofy stuff like *Our Town*, where the dead people get to come back from the grave and watch life going on without them. As I looked at Pleasant Valley, I couldn't tell, for a moment, if what I was seeing was the past or the present or the future.

"We're not doing anything illegal," said Dad. "We can park here and look."

"We can even get out and walk around and look," Clara said.

At that, even my dad hesitated.

"Come on," said Clara. "I'm not doing this alone."

My dad and I got out. We shuffled around for a while, and finally, when we got up the nerve, we went right up to the windows. It was a modern, one-story school, so we could see into practically every room.

It was completely dusty and deserted. But there was none of that quiet, sleepy feeling you got from a school on Sunday or after hours, when everyone had gone home. It looked as if it had been abandoned in a terrific hurry. There were open books on some of the desks, backpacks in the aisles. The lab tables were covered with half-finished science experiments. If you used your imagination, you might almost think that those vials and beakers were still bubbling and fizzing. Like Silas and Avery, the redheaded kid had been right. All his worst fears had come true. They'd come and gotten the last kids in the middle of a normal school day.

We went from window to window. At first each of us went around on our own. But after a while we waited for one another, and stuck together. No one wanted to be alone.

Clara said, "There used to be a school here, there used to be kids here. And now they're just vanished. Gone. And no one's concerned, no one's accountable. They never even bothered to clean up the mess."

"I've seen enough," my dad said at last.

"Can we leave now?" I asked them.

Just at that minute, my dad's cell phone rang. He let it ring for a while. And then he answered.

"Oh, Dr. Willner!" he said. And then he said,

"Yes, I understand. I see. Of course."

My heart was pounding. How had he gotten my dad's cell phone number? Clara and I looked at each other, and though we didn't say a word—we were too busy listening, trying to figure out what Dr. Willner and Dad were saying—it was as if Clara and I were having a parallel conversation.

Finally my dad said, "Sure. Sure. See you then. Good-bye."

"What did he want?" I said.

"He wants to see you and me in his office tomorrow morning. He wants to discuss our inappropriate interest in Pleasant Valley."

"How does he know?" asked Clara. "How did he know we're here?"

"I guess Big Brother's watching," said my dad.

Clara said, "I've never been so frightened in my life."

"But tomorrow's Sunday," I said. "He wants to see us *tomorrow*?"

"He said tomorrow," my dad repeated.

There was a silence. Then I said, "Are we going to his office tomorrow?"

My dad put his arm around my shoulders and pulled me up against him. "Not on your life," he said.

Driving back, no one talked. No one said a word.

When we were almost home, my dad said, "I think the important thing here is not to panic."

"Who's panicking?" said Clara.

"Yeah, who's panicking?" I said. Then we all laughed, and stopped laughing. We walked into our house. I wanted to call Becca and Brian right away, to tell them what I had seen. But I was afraid to call them or send them e-mail.

"I'll fix some lunch," said Clara, though it hadn't been very long since we'd eaten those big breakfasts. And no one was hungry. But maybe Clara wanted lunch. After all, she'd just had a bowl of oatmeal. I couldn't believe it used to annoy me that Clara ate food like oatmeal.

We stood around the kitchen. My dad pulled the curtains closed, and I found myself thinking about *Invasion of the Body Snatchers*.

Finally Clara said, "What now?"

"I don't know," my dad said. "Maybe the best thing would be to take a little vacation. Go away for the weekend. Put some distance between us and all this. Put ourselves in a more peaceful place so we can think all this over and regroup."

Did he really mean we were just going away for the weekend? The weekend was half over. But I was all for it, for getting out of town, even if just for a day, especially when my dad said, "Do you think any of your friends might want to go away for the weekend with us?" I thought of how my mom would often invite my friends along when we went places. It had been years since my family and I had gone anywhere with other kids.

I said, "Can we stop by Brian's and Becca's houses? On our way out of town?"

"Two is fine," my dad said. "After that we have to rent a bus. And I think it would be a little obvious."

"I only have two friends left," I said.

We decided to take Clara's minivan. It had way more room than the car. It said Green Land Nursery on the side, but so what? I was beyond worrying about riding in a vehicle that said something uncool. Of course it made us easier to find if anyone was looking for us. But somehow we didn't think it had gotten to that point yet. We didn't think anyone would come after us, as long as we didn't make any trouble

"Pack for a *long* weekend," my dad said. We knew what he really meant.

I packed some sweatshirts and jeans, and threw an extra pair of sneakers in my suitcase. I tossed in the stamp collection I'd gotten from my grandpa. I took the pictures of Mom from my desk, and the mask—the crazy rubber chicken mask—that she'd given me one Halloween, and the copy of *20,000 Leagues Under the Sea* that she'd read me when I was a little kid and that I'd thought was so dull. Maybe I would like it now. I threw it in my backpack, together with my Walkman and some CDs.

I told myself it was just for a long weekend. That was the only way I could do it without starting to cry.

First we stopped at the bank, at the drive-thru window. Dad and Clara withdrew the maximum amounts on their ATM cards. Then we went to Brian's house. The Land Rover was not in the driveway. I went inside anyway.

Brian was there, and I got him. It took him about two minutes to pack, that's how quickly he got with the program.

I said, "Do you want to leave your parents a note?"

"I don't think that would be such a great idea," he said. And his eyes filled with tears. I'd never seen Brian cry before; I didn't think he ever did.

But I suppose that everyone does. It just takes something sad enough.

I was really nervous as we drove toward Becca's house. Becca's mom answered the door. When she saw me, and looked around and saw Clara's minivan behind me, I got the strangest feeling that she understood what that was happening. Maybe that was part of being a mom. Which was something I wouldn't have known about.

Becca's mom let me in and called Becca. Then she went into the kitchen.

Becca looked as if she hadn't slept either. Her hair was dirty and sticking up in little blond points. I realized that she was still totally freaked about being caught with the paint, and she didn't even know yet about our field trip to Pleasant Valley.

I explained things to Becca as best I could—how my dad and Clara and I had driven out there this morning, and the phone call my dad got from Dr. Willner when we stood outside the Pleasant Valley school, and how he'd wanted to see us tomorrow. She didn't need convincing. She knew we were in danger.

I didn't know what she said to her mom. It didn't take very long.

A moment later Becca's mom came out of the kitchen. She said, "I'm going with you."

"Don't you want to wait for Dad?" Becca said.

"Dad will catch up," said her mom. "We'll figure out how to reach him. There isn't time now."

We all got into Clara's minivan and pulled out onto the highway. After a couple of hours, my dad took over the driving. Clara sat in the passenger seat, staring straight ahead.

And once she reached around behind her and took my hand and squeezed it.

I squeezed back.

Brian napped, and then Becca fell asleep, too. Becca's mom stared out the window, and once, when I looked back, I saw that she was crying. I wondered if she were worried about Becca's dad. Would Dr. Willner want to talk to him when he found out Becca was gone? But so far, there was no evidence that parents were in danger. It was only kids they were after, kids they wanted to control, or—failing that—kids they wanted to get rid of.

I stayed awake the whole time.

Clara and Dad talked softly.

No one knew where we were going, though we seemed to be heading west. Maybe to California. Canada, if we had to. Alaska. I liked the snow. I could deal with the cold.

We'd have to see how things turned out. We knew what we had to find. We had to find a place where we could live, where we could still be happy. Somewhere that hadn't been ruined yet. Someplace where there was peace. Somewhere where no one had ever heard about Pleasant Valley, or about what happened after.